SPOILED LUNCH
And Other Creepy Tales

By A.E. Hodge

A Fiction Fugitive Select Publication

For Melissa

*Text, cover, and interior images copyright © 2013
by Anthony Edward Hodge*

www.aehodge.com

ISBN: 0615868738
ISBN-13: 978-0615868738 (Fiction Fugitive Select)

TABLE OF CONTENTS

Acknowledgments

Special thanks to Melissa Mueller, Jamie Lybarger, and Phil and Carla Hodge, all of whom inspired me, encouraged me, and contributed in other ways—not only to this publication, but to my incubation as a writer. Without you this collection would not have been possible. Thank you.

Introduction

In this collection, a hungry child in a post-apocalyptic wasteland seeks shelter in the wrong place (*The Rollerboard*); a school boy in a dystopian world plagued by deadly pests learns to follow the rules the hard way (*Spoiled Lunch*); a ghost refuses to leave her beloved house (*The Agoraphobe*); a heroin addict finds himself trapped in a locker room with a talking tapeworm (*In the White Room*); two men on a hunting trip have a personal encounter with the supernatural (*The Hunters*); a drug runner hits a creature on the road and finds himself pursued by it (*The Accident*); a test subject in a secret government program learns the true meaning of his migraines (*The Migraine*); and a girl tries to rid her family's house of a ghost with disastrous results (*Sold As Is*).

The Rollerboard

As the toxic sun settles in its apex over the wasteland, you stumble upon what was once some kind of way station: now it is a midden heap of broken bricks and scattered debris, burnt-out cars and twisted gasoline pumps; a relic of prehistoric America.

You don't want to get any closer. You know what sort of surprises nest in the cool, dark places: scorpions, sand-wizards, mad mutant cannibals. After all, you are but a child, weak and weary, defenseless since losing your knife against the wild dogs in Reno.

But the hunger cannot be swayed.

You can't remember the last time you ate. Perhaps it was the dead dog, on the broken road outside Old Vegas. Or the nectar of that sickly green cactus, rich with radiation. But that was days ago, or months. Time seems endless and unsegmented under the white-hot sun. There are no clouds, no ozone, no atmosphere to shade the ultraviolet. There is only the sun, and the hunger, a constant twisting knife in your stomach.

It's the hunger that drives you closer.

You creep over the splintered asphalt, past twisted metal and shells of car parts from some other world.

Enter the dusty, cave-like doorway, into cool darkness. Shards of glass underfoot announce your every step. There are rows of dented, empty shelves inside, many of them fallen, their contents scattered. Rows of fluorescent lights, long dead, line the cracked and slanted ceiling.

You root through the debris with the toe of your boot: cardboard boxes, rotten packages, scraps of candy wrappers and empty cans—but no *food*. The packages have all been opened, the food long gone.

You hope whatever opened them isn't still around.

Outside, the desert wind lifts its voice two octaves. The walls shake. The ceiling groans. A storm is coming, one of the great and endless wind-storms that now circle the globe.

Finally you notice a rusted steel crate, half-concealed under ash and debris near the cashier's counter. The crate bears a faded red cross and script in an old language—*EMERGENCY RELIEF*—and your heart leaps up because you've seen these crates before. Every survivor has seen these crates. They hold a liquefied algae-based food source from the old world, renewable and nearly endless in shelf-life. *Manna*, they call it. It is the single most valuable substance left in the world.

With a cry of delight you fall on the crate, spilling it over eagerly.

But all that remains inside is a crib of fat grey ash-worms, each the size of your finger, moist and plump and sallow. The white spots on their heads look like startled eyes. You recoil in disgust and disappointment—but that's simply instinct. At this point you'll settle for anything.

The ash-worms slide down your throat so easily you almost can't taste the oily gasoline flavor.

But it's not enough. Indeed, it seems to only whet your appetite, honing its sharp insistency.

You search behind the counter and discover a small trapdoor in the wooden floor, perhaps to a cellar. It fills you with unease, but hunger saps your better judgment, and besides, there's a storm on the way. Where else can you go? Pull open the rust-hinged hatch. Swing over the lip. Descend down the step ladder into darkness.

The shaft below, hewn out of the black desert earth, seems to plunge down a long way. This is no mere cellar, as you'd hoped. It feels like a throat, and you are climbing down into the stomach of the hungry earth.

Your foot touches the bottom, and you turn around. With one hand to the rough wall, you walk tentatively into the utter darkness, your footsteps echoing. You can see nothing, and you have never felt more naked. Any moment your groping hand could land on some poisonous crawler, or a hole could open up in the floor and break your leg.

But the darkness decreases the further you go; suddenly you can discern the uneven walls, their recesses and stalactite pillars. Some curious dim light is coming from beyond a turn ahead.

You creep around the corner, into a little room. On one wall is a slender tube, glowing, not by electricity, but by some inner chemical source of its own. In its light, you see that this room is a residence: there are boxes and empty cans, torn garments, a blanket, a traveling pack...

At the back of the room is a cot; on it, a supine figure.

This residence is occupied.

You nearly panic and run, but then you see something else—there, beside the cot, lies a dead rat.

Instantly you start to salivate, and your stomach lurches hungrily. You can smell the sickly pungent smell of meat from here. You can't leave it behind. And the sleeper has not yet alerted to your presence.

It'll be easy: creep in, swipe the rat, and make a break before the stranger even stirs. You brace yourself, and then start forward, careful that your worn-down boots make no sound.

But you see at once that caution is unnecessary. The thing on the cot is a skeleton, its flesh long gone to dust. Only the clothes and blanket draping it give it shape.

You stumble to the rat, a tiny, malnourished thing, and seize it with trembling hands. With no hesitation you bite into its soft underbelly, wrenching away a great mouthful of meat, spitting out the skin and fur. The body is still fresh, only just turning cold. Blood dribbles down your chin. You can taste the sweet innards, the dry tough wires of muscle. This simple pleasure is unsurpassed.

In a matter of moments you've gummed and chewed the flesh from the rat's skeleton, and it looks almost as clean and picked as the human skeleton on the cot. Your jaw is sore from exertion, and in the spaces between your many missing teeth, your gums are bleeding from gnawing the bones.

But still the pains gnaw your stomach, the tiny scraps of rotten meat only serving to stoke your feeding frenzy.

Where did the rat come from?

The cave-like tunnel continues on from this small chamber, crawling down into darkness; was there more meat to be found?

You sit upright and listen, but hear nothing save the wind squealing through the building above. No reason to be afraid. No harm in exploring.

Maybe there will be more food.

God, you need food.

You pry the glowing light-stick from the wall. The strange inner glow dims, but does not go out. You clutch it like a talisman and start down the sloping tunnel, waving the glow-stick to ward off anything living in the dark; but the cave seems strangely empty of scorpions, insects, or other creatures.

Every step is nervous and jumpy. Your senses, honed by past danger, blare like warning sirens, but you can't turn back.

On the way down, you pass another opening in the tunnel wall, dark like the mouth of a void. Tread lightly, but don't turn back, even if your heart is suddenly racing here and you can't say why. Just flee onward.

Soon after, you hear the drip of water. Then the passage opens into a circular chamber. The rock floor is wet; water trickles from a spring in the wall, down into an old moldy bucket. You bring the bucket to your lips, and the taste of water is pure and sweet, not oily, as you've grown used to in this dead world. You sip slowly; it's a struggle not to chug it, but there's no use making yourself sick.

Finally nervousness makes you lower the bucket and look around the little chamber. You listen. The storm is rising; the sound of squealing wind is loud enough that it seems right behind you now.

Time to go back, before you scare yourself mad down here. You set the bucket down to collect the trickle again, and then start up the tunnel. Echoes of your footfalls follow.

You come again to the opening in the tunnel wall, and slow to a stop. This is the source of your fear. Like a frightened deer, you stare into the dark crevice for a long moment, and then try to run past.

The squealing sound gives chase—not the sound of wind at all, but of wheels—and you look back and some monstrosity is squeezing from the dark crevice, eyes glittering, teeth grinning—

And it's coming for you, a corpulent thing rolling with grotesque agility on a plywood board on wheels, scrabbling along on its palms, dragging its trunk and the stumps of old legs, coming toward you with a stupid malevolent grin in a face like melted wax, and one of its flapping hands is leading ahead like a feeler, seeking to touch you, and when it does you'll go insane.

Screaming, you make it to the room at the end of the tunnel— and stumble over the skeleton on its cot, twisting your ankle with a lightning arc of pain as you go down. You claw your fingers into the hard ground and drag yourself away, but you're too slow, far too slow.

"No!" you scream. "No!" Your eyes squeeze shut, unable to watch.

The cold cave-hand clamps on your leg, and by reflex you kick with all your strength. There is a groan of pain muffled as if by cotton, and the hand subsides. You open your eyes. The monster lies on its side; the rollerboard, kicked out from under it, is rolling back down the tunnel.

You kick the monster till it half-rolls, half-drags itself away from you, snuffling and grunting like a dog; it turns, and under the faint glow of the light-stick, it looks at you with eyes that are hungry—but human. You see that *it* is a *he*—not a true monster at all, but a disfigured, crippled man in the last stages of some rotting sickness. You cannot flee;

all you can do is look into those old, filmy eyes.

Eyes so like your own.

The mutant opens its crooked jaws; foamy drool spatters from its mostly toothless mouth. "Jeh," it says. "*Jeh.*" It props itself upright with one hand and slaps its chest with the other.

You realize it's telling you its name.

The voice is so hoarse and distorted that the word could be almost anything—Jim, Jeff—but it sounds to you like *Jeb.*

You demand to know what it wants. Your voice wavers with fear, but you try to sound forceful, threatening.

In response, the creature tries to crawl closer.

"No!" you scream, kicking away. "No, stay back!"

But there's no need to panic. The Jeb-thing is too sick and weak to drag its fleshy body without the rollerboard, and when you shout at it, the Jeb-thing stops trying, its eyes abashed as a beaten dog's.

You inch a little closer yourself, carefully; your throat is too hoarse to shout from afar. You look past the Jeb-thing at the skeleton, beneath its blanket, and ask, "Did you eat him?"

The Jeb-thing shakes its head with child-like vigor—but is that guilt in its eyes?

"What about the cans of food?" you ask. "Is there any left? Or more rats? Anything?"

It shakes its head mournfully. The hunger grows in what's left of its expression.

You can hear how hard the storm is raging above. You cannot leave this underground refuge, not till the storm abates. But how can you stay now, here with this creature? How can you be sure you won't wake to its biting teeth?

You study the mutant and it returns an abject, guilty gaze. There is something strangely infantile in it.

Just what is the nature of this beast? Does it know sadness? Loneliness? Does it know its own hideousness? Perhaps this Jeb-thing was once a healthy human boy, a vessel brimming with dreams. Perhaps it was once a father. Perhaps you remind it of its *own* child from long ago, and when its fumbling hand tried to touch you it was only to caress you.

But there is also the dead body to consider, and the creature's hungry eyes.

"Stay where you are," you tell it, "and I'll stay where I am. And when this storm's gone I'll go on my way and leave you in peace. Understand?"

Jeb-thing only returns its vacant smile. You'll have to hope this is agreement enough.

Your stomach groans as if to punctuate the discussion. Dull pain aches in your middle. Now comes the waiting, and the watching.

Minutes turn to hours, hours to days. Hunger growls in your belly and now in your mind, crippling your thoughts with its predatory jaws. All the while you dare not take your eyes from your strange companion. The Jeb-thing looks over at you, too, its eyes mournful and awkward and—longing? Lustful? Hungry?

It's going to eat you. If you close your eyes for even a moment, it will scramble up and eat you.

The thought of consumption does not just terrorize you: somehow, it hones your own appetite. It twists the knife of hunger. It is *food* you need, *food* that called you into this freak house. It is want of food that will slowly kill you, if the Jeb-thing doesn't first.

Try to occupy your mind, try to focus on something, anything. Your thoughts are made vivid by fear and fever—but your hunger is just as vivid, just as sharp, and you can't focus.

And the thing is going to eat you.

You look over at it. It grins back at you; the few crooked teeth in its rotting mouth have been ground down to sharp, sharky points. Those fangs will tear your flesh as easily as razor blades.

All the while, starvation saps your strength, compelling you to weariness. Your eyelids grow heavier, your breathing deeper. Your fingertips feel numb. But you *mustn't* go to sleep. It'll eat you for sure.

Your eyes begin to close, and you sit bolt upright, slap your cheeks to wake up. Now you look over; Jeb-thing is smiling; and doesn't it seem closer to you than before?

You warn it to stay back. Your voice is slurring. Too much

hunger, too much—

It's going to eat you.

The Jeb-thing grins back. The childishness has dripped away; that grin is unafraid, in control, hungry.

You kick at it. "Get back, I'm warning you!" No movement. You inch closer, kick again. "Get back! I'll... I'll kill you if I have to! I'll *kill* you!"

And what would you do with the body?

You clutch a hand to your aching head. The world has begun to spin. Cold pain tingles at the base of your spine. How much of this pain and madness would end if you could just eat—

before you're eaten

—something, *anything*, God, you're losing your mind, and the Jeb-thing is getting closer, you know it, closing in slow and stealthy, closing in while you suffer, while you're weak, and now you feel its cold mutant fingers on your ankle, and then its wet lips kissing—*tasting*—your dry, blistered skin.

You scream and lunge at the Jeb-thing, smashing your fist into its skull, which gives like mushy, overripe fruit. Jeb-thing falls backward, howling, "*Eeze! Eeze!*" but you chase it, pummel it, kill or be killed. It's fighting back, flailing and whimpering and snarling. Its old nails dig deep furrows in your skin. One slash hits your eye and you go half-blind with blood and fury; you bear down on the Jeb-thing with all your weight, find its throat, and squeeze, squeeze, squeeze—

"Eeze!" Jeb-thing rasps. "Eeze, no! Pore..."

Its last desperate flails graze your cheeks. Blood runs over your lips and the taste incenses you, drives you to finish, tears falling from your eyes.

When Jeb-thing stops moving and its blue eyes go out, you'll lean back with a pained wince and maybe crawl away, still weeping, feeling as much guilt as relief. But it had to be done; for your own safety, and your sanity. Anyone would understand.

You'll try to throw up at first, and for a while only dry-heave. Maybe you'll spit up some yellowish phlegm, mingled with bright blood from the tumors incubating in your lungs.

You're dying—just like everything else—and you're beginning to feel it.

You'll crawl a little closer to the Jeb-thing. You'll prod at it, test its consistency. The body is fleshy, bloated in the extremes of its sickness. And the pain will murmur in your empty stomach.

What *will* you do with the body?

I suppose you've known all along.

Some time later—days, months, years, who can tell?—you hear something moving upstairs. The storms have died long ago, but you can't leave this place, not with your ankle broken and your mind broken and your body sick and poisoned and bloating. You cannot leave this place; so here you lie, waiting; a prisoner left behind after all the wardens are dead.

And now you think you hear something. You wheel in the rollerboard—it helps you move these days—a little further up the dark, dank tunnel, past the picked skeleton of the Jeb-thing. You wheel almost all the way to the ladder that leads upward, before you hear for certain, and yes:

Something is moving upstairs. Something—or *someone*. Yes, you pray it is some*one*, pray someone new has stumbled upon the way station. You've been so desperately lonely.

And hungry.

Spoiled Lunch

"Now, don't you dare open this bag until lunchtime. You hear?"

Neil nodded as he took the zippered lunch bag from his mom. Her high heels clopped on the hardwood floor as she waddled around the kitchen, making last-minute preparations for work. Neil waited beside the front door, staring through the small panes of reinforced glass at the sidewalk and the road, bright in the morning sun. The weather, air quality and pest reports droned on the flat screen in the living room.

The yellow school bus rolled up outside. "It's here!" Neil called, settling his backpack on his shoulders. "Bye, mom!"

He turned the handle and the hydraulically-sealed front door opened, hissing as the vacuum released. His mother shuffled after him, breathing heavily, her fat cheeks red with blush and exertion. "Have a good day, honey." She patted his shoulder, but he dodged out the door before she could lean in for a kiss, as she sometimes did—despite that *everyone* on the bus could see.

After the crypt-like cool of the house, the May morning air felt hot and damp. The woods on the edge of the subdivision buzzed with insects, competing with the drone of electric lines. The sun felt especially hot through the broken ozone today. He hurried down the short sidewalk and bobbed up through the open bus doors, which closed behind him with the same vacuum-tight seal.

He plopped down in his accustomed seat near his friends Rachel and Josh from up the road. "What's up Fat Neil?" said Josh, popping up from the seat behind him. Rachel smiled from across the aisle. The bus pulled away with a growl.

"Did you finish the biology assignment?" Rachel asked. "We couldn't figure it out. I think Roberts gave us the wrong page numbers."

"Okay, good, so I'm not going crazy," said Neil.

He'd known both Josh and Rachel through all of elementary school, and now in fourth grade they shared most of their classes. It made splitting up homework convenient, though Josh rarely pulled his weight. Neil didn't mind. As long as he could help Rachel.

"Whatcha got for lunch, Fat Neil?" Josh said. He always called him *Fat Neil* because they knew another slightly trimmer Neil at school; but Josh himself was hardly slim.

"Tuna-Ish sandwiches," Neil said uneasily. Tuna-Ish™ was a proprietary blend of protein compounds designed to replicate real tuna fish.

"Ooh. Risky." Josh grinned.

Neil held up the air-tight lunch bag. "I can't smell anything. Do you?"

"All I got's ChocoPacks," said Josh. "Stupid dad didn't get anything. Wanna trade?"

"We're not supposed to open lunches outside the cafeteria," said Neil.

"That's a school rule," said Josh. "We ain't at school yet. Anyway, the bus is air-tight. I know you like ChocoPacks."

"I don't want to get in trouble," said Neil.

"Chicken." Josh sneered.

"Leave him alone," said Rachel.

Neil blushed. They rode in silence the last few minutes to school. There, the bus backed up to one of the loading docks at the back of the building. The gates rolled open with a hiss and the bus driver opened the emergency door at the back of the bus. The children trundled out one by one onto a conveyor belt that took them deeper into the school.

Almost every child was as fat as Fat Neil, and a few were even fatter. According to Mr. Roberts, the country's obesity rates were now over eighty percent, thanks in part to huge holes in the food web. Over the past fifty years, large portions of the ecosystem had been killed off from the bottom up. Climate change, combined with rapidly evolving viruses and pests, had wiped out entire species, and left little access to fresh, healthy food, beyond what could be engineered in a research lab and manufactured in a corporate factory.

This had been the subject of Mr. Roberts' lesson all week, and he continued it today—after apologizing for the mistake in the homework assignment—with a discussion of the so-called super-pests. "In addition to mass die offs in the animal kingdom, human agriculture was further hindered by the evolution of certain pests. These species, largely scavengers, largely insects, became adapted to the changing environment more readily than other creatures, and rapidly expanded in population in the absence of many predator species."

Josh whispered to Neil that the super pests were a myth, since he'd never seen them before. Neil tried to ignore him and focus on the biology lecture. He'd eaten three EggWites™ this morning, hoping that would be enough to see him through to lunch for once, but he was already getting hungry. Josh and his stupid ChocoPacks™.

"Of particular note among these super-pests," Mr. Roberts continued, "are the *Plecia maxima*, of the family *Bibionidae,* more commonly known as 'the black flies'." The rotund old teacher pushed a button on his computer, and the slick 3D image on the massive flat screen at the front of the classroom changed to a microscopic detail of the head of a fly.

"Although similar in appearance to the common horse-fly, the black flies are not blood drinkers, but rather scavengers and herbivores. They do not eat the living, but they are nevertheless lethally dangerous due to the tremendous size of their swarms…"

Rachel passed Neil a note. *Not sure what's worse, that fly or Roberts bald head.* Neil giggled and smiled at her.

Before he could write back, the bell rang and the class period came to a close. Mr. Roberts hurriedly gave them a homework assignment and ushered them off to their next class. In the hallway, Josh poked Neil from behind. "Hey, chicken," he said. "You want to see if these black flies are real or not?"

"Of course they're real," said Neil. "We wouldn't be learning about it in school if it weren't true. Besides, all the rules…"

"You scared of breaking a few rules?" said Josh, just loud enough for Rachel to hear. When her eyes met Neil's, she looked away. Neil's face reddened and he turned toward Josh.

"Shut up. I'm not chicken."

"So let's have some of that sandwich, then," said Josh. His face was surprisingly sympathetic. The boy was truly hungry; his careless father had likely forgotten his breakfast as well as his lunch. Then, seeming to realize his own transparency, Josh shrugged like he couldn't care less. "Unless you're scared of a few black flies…"

Neil was starting to get irritable. "How many ChocoPacks you got?"

"Three," said Josh.

Neil's stomach rumbled mournfully at the thought of the delicious pudding. "How about this," he said. "I'll give you one of the sandwiches for all three ChocoPacks."

"No way!" said Josh. "One pack per sandwich."

"One Tuna-ish sandwich is worth more than one ChocoPack," said Neil. "It ain't even worth it for just one. But I mean, if you're really going hungry, I guess you could owe me," he added, sarcastically.

Josh's nostrils flared. "How about *this*," he said, "I'll give you all three ChocoPacks, if *you* eat one of your precious sandwiches outside."

Neil blinked. That was unexpected. His heart was already racing with the adrenaline of laying his reputation on the line with Rachel here watching him. Josh knew it, too. He stood there smirking, knowing Neil wouldn't rise to the challenge.

But Neil had been putting up with Josh's needling for too long, and in front of Rachel, it was too much. He couldn't back down. "You give me three ChocoPacks today, and bring me two more tomorrow," said Neil.

Josh laughed. "Yeah right. You wouldn't dare."

Neil came to his locker and stopped, looking around to make sure no one was watching before he grabbed his lunch from inside, stuffing the air-tight bag under his shirt. He glared at Josh. "Five ChocoPacks. Deal?"

Josh rolled his eyes. "Yeah, sure. If you actually do it, sure. You ain't gonna do it."

Neil led the way toward an emergency exit. He knew the alarm there was disabled as he'd seen teachers going out that way on smoke breaks. He stepped out into the bright hot daylight. The perimeter of the school, including the athletic yard, was screened in completely against pests; but at the back was a small gate to an open meadow.

"Neil," said Rachel, "if you're trying to impress me…"

His face reddened. "I'm not," he snapped. "They're just flies.

They don't even eat the living. I'm hungry, damn it."

But now, as he crossed the blacktop toward the gate in the mesh screen fencing, he found he wasn't hungry at all. But he wouldn't back down. His father had been stubborn, too, his mother always said so.

"Whoa, Neil," Josh said finally, as they reached the gate. "She's right, man. Forget it. You don't have to do this. I'll give you two ChocoPacks for one sandwich. That's fair."

But Neil was already opening the gate, stepping out into the meadow. Josh closed the gate behind him, looking astonished and fearful through the mesh. Neil liked that look on Josh's face for once. No, there was no turning back now. The balance of power had suddenly changed, and Neil was too high on it.

"What's wrong, Josh?" he laughed. "Who's the chicken now?"

"He's not serious," Josh said. "He's not serious. Come on in, man. We're not buying it." But there was a strange nervousness in his voice.

Neil went a few yards out into the open meadow, under the blaring sun, and then turned back to his friends. Ignoring their protests, his heart pounding, Neil unzipped his lunch bag and pulled open the air-tight cap inside.

He removed the Tuna-ish from its plastic baggie, held the smelly sandwich in trembling hands in the open air.

And nothing happened.

He breathed a sigh of relief and looked up at Josh. "See?" he cried triumphantly. "Who's the chicken now?"

Rachel laughed and Josh broke into a nervous smile. Neil took a bite of his sandwich, and instantly his appetite roared back, and he started eating it furiously.

As he ate, a single fly buzzed around his head. He laughed and swatted at it. His friends laughed too. So much for the super-pests.

Then the fly landed on the bread. That nauseated him, but he swatted it away.

Then he realized it was not one, but three different flies buzzing around him, loud and fat. Or was it more than three?

All the while, he'd begun to notice a sound from the woods on the edge of the meadow, at first so low it was almost beyond hearing, but growing steadily and imperceptibly into a dull, blaring drone. He felt cool suddenly, and realized his friends were shouting again, their voices diminished by the droning buzz, and a shadow passed over the sun.

Three flies suddenly became three hundred, swarming over the entirety of the sandwich in his hand. He threw it down and a thousand flies swarmed it, and in seconds the sandwich vanished, devoured, as if it had never been.

Neil dropped his lunch bag and stumbled away through the black cloud, swatting, his eyes squeezed shut. He kept running until he struck the mesh fence. Only when he opened his eyes did he realize the gate was several yards away.

But the flies weren't swarming him, he realized. They were swarming around his lunch. They formed a tight column over the lunch bag on the ground, funneling down toward it like a thick black cyclone.

It was the food they wanted, not him. They didn't eat the living. They only ate the dead.

He started to laugh in a high, thin, hysterical voice. "Stupid flies!" he cried. "I ain't scared of you! I ain't scared of nothing!"

Even as he spoke, he noticed a faint smell of tuna fish. The buzzing flies seemed to pause in mid-air, as if noticing as well. Instantly he realized he should've never opened his mouth.

Because Neil still had a serious case of tuna breath.

No sooner had he finished the last word than he felt a fly buzz into his mouth. He snapped his jaw shut, crunching the fat fly in his teeth. More flies swarmed his face, touching his lips, flying at his nose, desperate to reach the source of the tuna smell. He pressed his lips together and closed his eyes—and next thing he knew he felt them buzzing up his nostrils, crawling in his ears. They were in his hair, in his shirt, they were climbing up his pants. He stumbled away and when he screamed they filled his mouth, faster than he could chew—and when he hit the ground and hid his face they wriggled up between his legs, finding other ways inside him there.

He felt them in his intestines. He felt them in his throat. He felt them finally in his stomach, crawling, expanding him. As he writhed in pain and rolled over the grass now black with flies he was moaning but it came out in a thin gargle, drowned, and when he sucked in air he was choking on them, drawing them into his airways.

When he looked down at his stomach it was bulging as if pregnant under his tee-shirt, things moving inside skin stretched tight as a snare drum. He felt something break inside him, felt blood spreading out from his belly button as he ruptured, blood soaking the tee-shirt, blood and the great black flies.

He deflated then, felt them leaving him, emptied and bleeding out from every orifice and a few new ones besides, his belly sagging like a burst balloon. The flies buzzed around him, hovering, as he faded. They were waiting, he knew, for the meal to resume—the main course. They didn't eat the living. They only ate the dead.

The wait wouldn't be long.

The Agoraphobe

It's hard to leave the house when you're dead.

Not that I ever left it much in life. Ever since I was a girl, my home was everything. There were boys and girls in the neighborhood—such cruel little children. I could watch them play in the street through the window, and feel like I was one of them without facing their cruelty. And when Mom and Dad were still together, when me and my little brother Eric were in school, we all had dinner in the grand dining room under the hammered bronze chandeliers.

Then, of course, my parents divorced, and Eric moved out, and I stayed here with Mom until her sickness. I must've been twenty, twenty-one when she passed. By then Dad was remarried, Eric gone away to Europe. Nothing left but this, this house. Of course with the money Mom left, I never had to work again. I could spend every day here, in peace, watching the world through the beautiful colors of the stained glass windows. So much better than *interacting* with the world. Dealing with people and their stupidity. My dad's drunken womanizing. Eric and Toula, his insipid little wife, always trying to set me up with that oaf George, that's her cousin. He has the palsy. High-functioning, mind you, but still. Just insipid. The way they're always over here, pawing at me for money for their little brats on every Hallmark holiday, like I should be guilty that Mom left everything to me! The way Eric chose Dad in court, he got what he had coming.

Oh, I had callers, mind you. The mailman, Theodore, we became close for a time. One of my neighbors, a married man. And that friend of my maid's, what was it—Ronaldo? The maid was a dirty immigrant thief, but Ronaldo—oh, but men only want one thing. Once they've puffed you down like a cigarette they snuff you out and move on to the next.

And I heard the rumors, of course. Saw the way kids stared up at the house when they passed on the sidewalk below. The weird lady, they called me. The witch.

Children can be so cruel.

And then one day I'm eating my oats and drinking my tea like normal, and all the sudden I can't move my arm anymore, and my vision clouds up, and just like that I drop like a fly, dead before I hit the ground. After all the morning yoga, all the disgusting fruit smoothies and, oh, the wonderful anti-oxidants, there I was, dead of a stroke at the age of fifty-two.

It wasn't some magical event, like they tell you in stories. No flashbacks of my life. No brilliant beams of light. I just—woke up. Found myself standing over my own body, looking at my head split open on the kitchen tiles, blood streaming from my nose. Here I was, back in my house. Where I belong. Where I've *always* belonged, in life and in death.

And you expect me to leave? Even if I could, you think I'd want to?"

I take a long drag of my cigarette, staring up at the beautiful hand-carved redwood rafters in the parlor. I lean over from where I lay on the sofa, flick the ashes in the ashtray on the mahogany coffee table, and spare Dr. Peter a sideways glance.

Peter sits on the covered loveseat across from me, studying the fat leather-bound journal in his lap, where he takes his notes. He adjusts his thin-framed reading glasses as he meets my eyes.

"I can tell this house represents a strong seat of security for you, Cindy." His voice is deep, calm, soothing. He looks to be in his late forties or early fifties, with a shining bald head and a close-cropped salt-and-pepper beard starting at his temples. His smooth skin and bright blue eyes make him seem younger. Uncommonly beautiful, but his type often are. "However," he says, "things aren't just about what *you* want."

"Oh, I know," I snap, sitting up on the sofa and putting out the cigarette in the ashtray. "This is *your* house now, right? You and your friend just want me gone."

"That isn't what I meant."

"No, no, it's fine," I insist. "You're right, after all. You must've paid good money for this place. Thinking you'd found the perfect home. Who'd have thought you'd be sharing it with the ghost of some old woman?" I laugh, the sound hoarse from smoking. "Tough luck, eh?"

At that moment the front door opens in the vestibule and I see the other one, Michael, coming in with shopping bags. He's younger, in impeccable fitness, his thighs and biceps bulging through his gym clothes like a Roman statue. His hair is long and golden, his eyes a bright green. He looks at us through the arched doorway of the parlor and frowns.

"You're still doing this?" he says.

Peter shrugs apologetically. "Just a little more time, I think," he replies. As if I'm not sitting right here.

"Hello to you, too, Mike," I say, with a wave.

He stalks away, shaking his head. Peter looks back at me gravely. "Cindy, we've been meeting for a long time now, and it's all been leading up to this. It's time to *break through*, Cindy. Time to leave the house."

"Listen, I do understand," I continue. "If I were alive and you two were the ghosts, I'd have called the exorcist by now. I really appreciate your meeting with me all these times, doctor, but I hope you're taking it for what it is. A case of mutual curiosity. If you're bored with me, I'm a *ghost*. I can make myself invisible. You'll never even know I'm here, I promise. If that's what you want. But I'm telling you, for the last time. I can't leave."

Peter smiles thinly. "Cindy, if you don't leave peacefully, Mike is going to have you removed. Today. And you won't like that."

Michael enters from the other side of the room, toward the kitchen, holding a plastic bag of crimson red candles. Without even acknowledging me, he sets them out on the coffee table in front of me in a semicircle, then begins to light them with a candle lighter.

I scowl. "You're bluffing."

"I wish I were," says Peter, with an apologetic shrug. "You've had plenty of opportunity to vacate of your own free will."

I rise to my feet. "Now you listen to me. I'm the one who's been patient here. I'm the one that's been graceful. If you want this to get ugly, I'm… more than ready."

Michael smirks as he lights the last candle and steps back. "It's too late for that."

With a sweep of my hand I carry a breeze through the parlor, flipping the pages of Peter's notebook, sending mail flying, tugging the sheer curtains of the windows—but the red candles do not so much as gutter. The five little flames remain unmoved. Furious, I do it again, and again, turning the room into a wind tunnel, to no avail.

"Please, Cindy," Peter protests, his white shirt rippling, his eyes blinking in the wind. "Just listen."

Instead I lunge for the candles, trying to knock them aside myself—but my hand stops against the first one, as if it weighs ten thousand tons. I try to kick the whole coffee table aside, and am unable.

"I'm starting the ritual," Michael tells Peter, who nods with a pained expression.

I glare at them, panting, slowly rising off the floor into the air. "You're making a mistake. You have no idea what I'm capable of. I will not leave this house."

I pass through the ceiling, into the upstairs hall, and stalk back into the master bedroom. *My* bedroom. It's hardly changed since I died—some of my belongings have been packed into dusty boxes, but the furniture, the stately canopied king-size bed, the solid oak armoires and dresser, all of it remains—I suppose I can thank Peter and Michael for that much, if nothing else, the treacherous bastards. I've been too friendly by half, it seems. Here I thought we could work together to make the best of an unpleasant situation, but if peace is off the table, I'll bring them war.

I snap my fingers and summon a power surge, blowing out every single light bulb in the house, one after another.

I make every mirror shatter.

I make spiders appear from every air register.

I make blood bubble up from every drain, spilling over the kitchen counter, filling the great claw-foot tub in the master bath, washing out over cerulean tiles.

We'll see how long these queers last against *me*.

When I turn around, Peter is standing in the doorway of the bedroom, wearing his usual pinched, anxious expression.

"You don't have much time," he says. "Once the ritual is complete, you'll be banished from this place. And you won't like where you end up."

I shriek in response and an ornate ceramic lamp streaks across the room. Peter moves his head to the side at the last moment and the lamp shatters against a far wall behind him. For a long moment I meet his eyes as I try to catch my breath, my hands squeezed into tight fists at my sides.

"Please, listen," Peter says. "When I told you it's not all about what you want, what I meant was... you have other people in your life. You do. You have... a father, a brother, a family that cares about you."

"They never cared," I snarl, "no more than you did. All of them... they were scum. Everyone is just..." I look down at my hands, clenching open and closed. "Just scum. I just want to be left alone."

"Cindy..."

"*Leave me alone!*"

The shutters all clatter and rattle. The floorboards creak and groan as if the whole house is swelling up with a great breath of air. The bedroom door slams in Peter's face with a sound like a gun blast.

Next thing I know I'm up in the attic, perched lightly on a rafter, my shoulders hunched with sobbing. This is why you can't trust people. Just when you're starting to open up, they turn around and stab you in the back. This is why it's better to be alone. Why everyone should just... go away.

I hold my breath and close my eyes, and far below, in the kitchen, the gasket on the gas line on the stove comes loose. Invisible propane starts to fill the blood-soaked room.

The trapdoor of the attic opens and Peter's head appears, his expression deeply concerned. "Aggression is a bad idea, Cindy. Besides, gas won't stop Michael."

I glare at him, bewildered. "Stop following me."

"What do you think will happen when that gas reaches Michael's candle?"

"You two faggots go boom?"

"And so does this house, and everything in it."

"It's in a historic district. They'll build it back to spec," I mutter, hiding my uncertainty. "If that's what it takes to be rid of you."

"There's something you need to know. I couldn't tell you sooner due to protocol. We... can't always be sure how humans in your situation will react."

"What are you talking about?"

He climbs the rest of the ladder up into the attic, dust-motes swimming around him. At the same time, through the floorboards, I hear Michael raise his voice in song far below, the words incomprehensible, chanting. The ritual.

"Cindy," says Peter. "You are not dead."

I shake my head and laugh. "Of course I'm dead, idiot. Last thing I remember is the stroke."

He gestures with his hands for me to calm. "You need to listen to me very carefully. There isn't much time. Right now you are very much alive, but that will all change unless you leave this house, *now*."

I stare at Peter, trying to make sense of this. It has to be a lie. Some final desperate deception. "If I'm alive, what the hell are you doing in my house?"

"This is not your house," says Peter. "All this, everything you see around you, was generated by your own mind. A coping mechanism, if you will. An attempt by a limited human mind to rationalize something incomprehensible to it." He turns and walks across the empty attic, to the small round window on the far wall. "Come, see for yourself."

I appear at his side, and he moves aside to let me look. At first I see nothing through the opaque sky-blue glass, but slowly I discern shapes outside, and realize I'm looking down into a wide sterile hospital room, far below. I see myself lying on a bed, a frail and wrinkled thing under sheets of white, so many wires and tubes spreading out from me it looks like I'm caught in a spider's web.

I raise a hand to hide my gaping mouth. "Impossible."

"I believe this is what you call a near-death experience," says Peter. "In your case, a much extended one. Most people come and go, or a loved one sends them back. But sometimes there are people who are so psychologically guarded, so *shut-in* to their very souls, that they can't be reached. They can't move on, and they won't go back; so they linger here, and hide, and wait, as they did in life, stuck in their own nexus place between life and death."

"If this is true," I whisper, "then who are you, and what do you want?"

Peter looks back at me, deadly serious. "We're angels, Cindy. We're trying to save you from yourself."

A tear rolls down my cheek. I fear I'm starting to understand, and the understanding is like a light in the corner of my mind, so bright I want to look away.

I sink back down into the parlor, lit in the eerie red of candlelight, where Michael faces the candles with his arms outstretched, as if beckoning something, crying out in Latin or something even older. "You've made your point," I scream at his vast muscled back. "I want to talk."

"Peter isn't lying," says Michael, and somehow the chanting goes on, seeming to swell out of the walls. "You're out of time. Either walk out the door—and choose life—or stay, forever."

Behind me something creaks, and I turn to see the front door swing open, hinges creaking with disuse. The light from beyond is too harsh to see through.

"How do I know that light goes back to Earth?" I ask.

"You don't," says Peter, suddenly behind me. "For once in your life, you have to trust someone."

"How do I know I'm all right, if I go back? How do I know I'm not crippled, or brain damaged...?"

"You aren't," says Peter. "I promise."

And I suppose I could trust them, these theoretical angels; could choose to believe. At worst, they've deceived me, and the light is the path to some uncertain afterlife, and I can never return home again. Or it could send me back among the living as they claim, and I'll wake from my coma on a hospital bed to—what? My demented father visiting from the nursing home? My brother and his wife and her oafish cousin George? All their passive aggressive concern, insisting I stay with them while they complain of the extra mouth to feed? The hospital bills? The therapy? The attention?

And if I stay here?

"When the ritual is complete, your soul will be severed permanently from the earthly world," Peter says urgently, as if reading my thoughts. "And you will be judged."

"Judged?"

"It's considered suicide. Choosing to go before your time. A deadly sin, I'm afraid. Again, protocol…" He opens his hands apologetically.

But something about his eyes reminds me of Maria, my former maid and housekeeper, the way she used to look when she lied through her crooked teeth at the end of the day, slipping off with another of my necklaces in her purse; or the way Renaldo used to look when he told me it was me, forever and ever, me and ten thousand others behind my back; of the children in my neighborhood growing up, the way they smiled as they hid the rocks behind their backs.

"No," I declare. "I don't trust you queers for a minute. *You* leave! This is *my* house, and I want you out—now!"

Peter sighs, and shakes his head; then he turns and walks out the front door.

Behind me, the next candle burns out, leaving only one remaining.

And then the gas reaches it.

There's a deep *whoomp* sound followed by the crash of every window blowing out and when I open my eyes the very air is filled with fire, every wall and surface turned to a carpet of flames. The curtains dance and shrivel into twisted black cords. Chips of paint and particles of plaster and smoke and ash blur the air.

Michael and I stand at the center of the inferno, both unfazed. He turns slowly to me, his smirk now somehow resigned. "Last chance," he offers.

"Do it," I say. "You don't frighten me."

He takes a step toward me and I shy back, but he only walks past calmly through the flames, and out into the light. He seems to change as the light meets him—for an instant, his silhouette spreads a vast pair of wings—and then is gone.

I walk to the coffee table, which stands untouched, as if surrounded in a protective force-field. The last candle is burned down to a red puddle, the flame guttering, guttering…

When the candle dies, the other flames wink out too with a hiss, like a gas grill turning off. The parlor is restored to its former state—the air clear, the walls and furniture undamaged, the glass in the windows intact. Just the same as the day I died. After the roar of the fire, the silence seems thick and deafening.

I turn to close the front door—but it's already closed. The light from outside is gone, and when I stand at the green Tiffany glass window beside the door, I can see nothing but my dim reflection in the gloom. I try to open the door, to see if Peter and Michael are still out there. The handle turns, but I can't open the door, as if it's melded into the wall. As if there is no door.

I drift from window to window through the silent empty house, but every window is opaque. When I try to open one in the kitchen, the latch is hot to the touch, and I spring back with a wince.

"Peter?" I call. "Michael?"

No answer. The house is empty. They're gone, truly gone. As the realization sets in, I begin to smile.

I turn on the record player in the sitting room and Bobby Darin's "Beyond the Sea" crackles out, ringing in the natural acoustics of the house. I move from room to room, dancing, vestibule to parlor to kitchen and dining and back, and up the steep semi-circular staircase to the second floor with its four great bedrooms and two baths, all mine again.

"Your little ritual back-fired," I declare. "You're gone, and I'm still here."

I drift into my bedroom and begin to unpack my belongings from their dusty boxes—the fine jewelry, the leather-bound books, the porcelain statues of animals and houses. "Finally some time to read," I say. "Finally have some time alone."

And when I run out of books? Then what?

I shove back the thought. "No more unwanted visitors," I continue. "No more distractions."

I take a mirror from a box and return it to its place on my dresser, staring at my own grinning face. They were wrong. Their ritual failed.

But something Peter said keeps echoing in the back of my mind. *You will be judged.*

"Is this your idea of judgment?" I say into the mirror. "Of *hell?* You couldn't be more wrong. Hell is other people. I get to keep the house I love, forever. And I never have to see another human being."

As I look at myself in the mirror, my smile begins to fade in a flicker of doubt.

"Forever."

Then the smile is gone.

In the White Room

The needle goes in, the blood comes out, the blood and the cool white heroin go back and then comes the chill and Joe leaves the floor of the locker room, sailing up and up, away from every stress and care. He feels them all slipping away, staying on the floor far below him.

Somewhere down there is his father's voice, still ranting at him. *No, I can't let you stay in a dorm room. No, you most certainly can't come home. We talked about this, Joseph. You can do what you want with your life, but you're not gonna screw up ours ever again.*

Joe leans his head against the locker room bench behind him, eyes glazed under heavy lids, the scene still fresh in his mind: standing in his father's office—the goddamn *Dean's* office—begging and pleading like a dog with the old bald bastard, but Dad it's five below outside and I'm out of doors and I might be coming down with something, and I've *told* you a thousand times I'm clean, forty-five days, God bless, and there must be *something*, Dad, something you can do for your ole first-born prodigal son. This humiliating little show, on and on, while Dad hemmed and hawed and scolded behind his vast oak desk and his checkered overpriced tie, finally sighing in resignation.

The gym's closed for renovations. I guess you could stay there a night. Just one night. Yes. The locker room. Don't act like you haven't stayed worse places. It's just tile in there, for whatever mess you make.

Just white tile, endless white tile and rows of stainless steel lockers and worn wooden benches, shower heads along the back wall. Around a corner is the restroom, then the door out to the empty campus gym. A handful of harsh fluorescents, the few not turned off for the winter, cast the room in stark light and sharp, angular shadow. The only color in the locker room is Joe—his lank blond hair, his ragged blue cardigan and cargo jeans sagging off his frame, his red sleeping bag rolled out beneath him.

He sets the needle on the bench beside him and spills backward over the sleeping bag like mercury, staring up at the white plaster ceiling. In the cool atomic chill of the high, nothing matters. His father's judgment, these poor accommodations, the faint smell of mold and dirty socks. Past, present, and future compress to a flat image on the TV screen of his brain, and then the picture fuzzes out.

Joe is flying. Floating on cool waves. He dreams of the past year spent on the street. He dreams of before, in his parents' home, going to school. He dreams of infancy, entombed in warm darkness waiting to be born.

Slowly his mind bobs back to his body, flicking along the surface like a skipping stone. He becomes aware of subtle pain in his rib cage, an old break, badly healed. He hears his breathing, deep, slow, and wheezing. His mouth is dry as cotton, his tongue throbbing and heavy, immovable. At the low edge of his bleary vision he detects something moving. Something itches at the back of his throat.

When he opens his eyes he sees the great pale body of something in his mouth, like a vast insect wriggling between his lips, crawling down his throat. He starts to choke and gag and then swallows, actually *swallows* it, then he lurches up from the floor and rushes around the corner to the restroom, slamming through a stall door and vomiting over the toilet, a thin spray of spittle and bile. He shoves his finger down his throat and tries to spit out more with great wracking dry heaves, but nothing comes, and there's nothing in the bowl. He stands above the toilet, gasping, his face a mess of tears and phlegm.

He talks to himself as he tries to catch his breath. Okay, okay, what was that? Is he hallucinating? Or did something actually crawl down his throat?

As if in answer, he feels a stab of movement in his guts, like bad gas resettling. He clutches his stomach in alarm.

That's when he tries to leave, to get to a phone, to a doctor, to anybody.

But when he stumbles into the big blue door at the front of the locker room, it bounces him back like a wall. He leans on the cold finished steel with all his frail weight and it doesn't budge. His eyes widen in disbelief. The door is jammed, or locked from outside.

"Oh come on," he cries. "You idiots locked me in?" He bangs his open palms on the door and shouts for someone to let him out, knowing the entire gym is empty for winter break and renovations. "Hey! *Hey!*"

He crawls back into the locker room, to his tattered backpack at the end of one of the aisles. He roots inside it until he finds the little pay-as-you-go cell phone, all he can afford since his parents cut him off. He pops it open. *No Signal.*

He stares at it for a while, hearing his own breathing echo in the dark space. He closes his eyes. Tries to calm himself. This was nothing, surely. Nothing was inside him. He was hallucinating. He'd done his first fix in over a day. He'd been saving it, his last hit. He was due for a bad trip. A bad come-down. A little paranoia.

He needs another fix, that's all, just to calm his nerves. He scrapes the bottom of his baggie, scrapes at his silver spoon, checks all the pockets of his backpack, but it's true. He's out. He meant to leave early this morning, meet his buddy Skunk with the hook up, but it appears he won't be going anywhere. Breathing in ragged gasps, he lurches back to the bathroom door and starts banging and shouting again, till his hand throbs and his voice goes hoarse and ragged.

His stomach lurches again, and he winces, tears coming into his eyes. This filthy room. His damn father. What kind of awful parasite has found its way into him? He remembers hearing that people on average swallow eight spiders a year in their sleep—what else did they swallow? The image of the great white wormy thing wriggling past his lips is imprinted on his mind.

It occurs to him how down he's been feeling lately, how slow and weak. Perhaps the creature was with him long before he came to this room. Perhaps Joe didn't witness it crawling in, but merely peeking out.

As his panic grows, he begins to hallucinate in earnest. The room changes. Things crawl along the walls. Shadows take strange forms at the corners of his eyes. He keeps hearing something tap-tap-taping, maddening. All the while his stomach cramps grow worse, moving steadily downward, the pangs of unease coming faster like contractions.

Then all at once something drops in his bowels and he rushes to the toilet stall, doubled over and moaning. Somehow he gets his pants down and sits before something bursts out of him, something not at all right. He cries out as it passes, wriggling down from his ass.

Instinctively Joe jumps aside as it splashes into the bowl beneath him. He backs up into the stall door, holding his pants up with one hand.

"Hey kid," says a voice from the toilet bowl, in a high-pitched New Jersey accent. "Ain't you gonna wipe?"

Joe stares, his mouth hanging open, as a pale worm creature lifts its head out of the bowl. The head is an inch wide, opening in a red mouth like a suction cup, encircled in small tentacles—or *teeth*. Beady black eyes, like a pig's, poke out to either side. It tilts its head to look at Joe, and the mouth twists into a smile.

A wordless moan escapes from Joe. He collapses to his knees, then his belly, and squirms backwards out from under the stall door, his eyes never leaving the worm. He keeps squirming till his back is pressed to the far wall, between two sink fixtures.

Inside the stall, the toilet flushes. "And not even the courtesy to flush," says the worm over the noise. "You've really embraced the whole *homeless* thing, ain't ya?"

"Oh man," Joe moans, running a hand over his sweat-drenched face. "This is one bad trip."

"You could've at *least* introduced yourself." The worm slithers out from under the door, and somehow it looks bigger than before, as thick as Joe's forearm and three feet long. It comes on like a king cobra, the front half of its body arched up. It fixes Joe again with its dead black eyes and eerie semblance of a smile. "Let me show you how it's done. I'm Tommy."

Tommy the talking tapeworm. Joe bursts into a manic giggle. He's hallucinating. He's in withdrawal. He just *needs a fix right now*. Ignoring the worm, he stands and goes back to banging on the sealed door at the front of the locker room and bellowing at the top of his lungs. "Let me out of here!" Hysterical laughter twists his voice, transforming gradually into sobs.

He hears Tommy slither up behind him. "Hey *Joe*," it says in a singsong voice. "Joseph? I'm talking to you, you rude son of a bitch."

"I don't want to hear it," Joe replies.

"You sure about that?" The worm pauses. Joe slowly looks back from the door. A few feet behind him, the worm tilts its head to meet his gaze with one eye. The eye narrows. "We got a problem here, you and I. And it's about time we discuss it."

"Tommy," Joe says, with a delirious smirk.

"Look," says the worm. "You may not even realize this, but I'm closer to you than anyone or anything in the world. Closer than your mudder. Closer than your pop. You're *special* to me, I'm saying."

"I'm your host," Joe says flatly. He eases down to sit with his back to the door.

The worm bobs its head in something like a shrug. "Your problems are my problems, is all I'm saying. Let me ask you something, buddy. When's the last time you ate?"

Joe looks down at his rail-thin frame, notices his pants are still unbuckled and corrects it.

"It's been days," Tommy answers for him. "And that was what, an 8-pack of McNuggets? I can't live off that crap. You realize that if *you* don't eat, *we* die, right?"

"Eating is about the furthest thing from my mind right now." Joe replies, feeling sick to his stomach. He puts his face in his hands. "I need to get out of here. I need to meet Skunk and get my stuff. And you need to cease to exist."

"Well," says the worm. It looks up and down at the door behind him. "You ain't going anywhere now that you went and fell for such an obvious trap."

"Trap?" says Joe, lifting his head. "What do you mean?"

The worm snickers, a dry, high-pitched sound. "You think that door just locked itself? This was a set up."

Joe understands instantly what the worm means. He hasn't even considered it before, *couldn't* consider it, but... "You think my dad locked me in here on purpose?"

"I can kinda understand his reasoning," says Tommy. "It's tough love. You clean out or you die. Only problem is, he trapped me in here too. And I *need* to *feed*. If we don't get out soon," it adds conversationally, "I may just eat you whole."

Joe barely hears this. A fresh kind of terror has settled over him. At first he refuses to believe it could be true, though he realizes it's been at the back of his mind all along. His father would starve him to death, drive him mad in here, leave him with Tommy as his final companion—

anything to force him to clean out. He chews his thumbnail, and then rises to his feet.

Joe goes back to the locker room and retrieves his backpack. He fishes through his meager provisions until he finds a rusted Boy Scout knife. He strides back to the locked door and flips open the blade and starts sliding it along the jamb of the door by the handle, trying to catch the latch.

"That ain't gonna work," Tommy comments from behind him.

Grunting, Joe tries to force it, and the rusted blade breaks off. He shrieks in rage and pounds on the door, then backs up and charges it, slamming himself against it. He keeps prying at the broken blade with his bare fingers, turning his fingertips to bloody shreds, but he can't get a grip.

"You definitely don't wanna do *that*," says Tommy. He fixes an eye on Joe's bloody hand. "You're really tempting me right now. You look like… mmm, like a big juicy wall of intestine."

Desperately Joe scans the room for any other exit, and his eyes land on a square outtake vent on the far wall of the bathroom, about two feet by two feet wide. He lunges for it, plucking at the screws on the grate, trying to get a grip on them with his bloody fingers, ripping his dirty fingernails.

"You'll never get in there either," Tommy says. "Why don't you calm down a minute? Come sit down and talk with me. Might be I got a solution to our mutual problem."

Joe looks back at the tapeworm, which cocks its head and grins. Joe leans back miserably against the dirty bathroom wall, trying to catch his breath and clear his head. The whole room is spinning. And the worm is right. He's weak, exhausted from hunger. He can't stay locked up in here. And he can't see a way out by himself.

He might as well talk to the worm.

He approaches it uncertainly. "So… Tommy, right?" he asks it, sarcastically. "How do I know you're really here? How do I know I'm not seeing things?"

Almost before Joe is finished speaking, the worm lunges like a spring across the room, its entire head seeming to open up into a gaping mouth, lined with rows of tiny teeth. It latches onto Joe's leg, clamping down through his pants. Joe yelps out in pain and tries to kick away—but the worm has already disengaged, slithering back, appearing almost to bow, as if pleased with its own performance.

"Jesus Christ," exclaims Joe, rubbing his leg, which is bleeding through his pants from the small round bite.

"Real enough for you?" asks Tommy.

"What are you?" demands Joe, staring at the worm in dull incomprehension. "If you're really here, what the hell are you?"

The worm tilts its head subtly, and its mouth twists again into a smile. "Do you really want to know?"

"How do you know my dad set this up?" Joe snarls.

"I know a lot of things," says the worm, still sneering. "I was with you when they kicked you out, you know. Dear old mommy and daddy. How well did they support you, when you needed help most? They put you out on the street, man, to live with ex-convicts and mental patients under that bridge on 7th Street. Yeah, I saw it. Everything you've been through. All on account of a little smack! If they'd do that to you, what *wouldn't* they do?"

Joe at first doesn't want to hear it, but by the end he finds himself listening to the worm very carefully. He finds the worm is making a lot of sense. It's true, his parents have disregarded his welfare before. But this… This is going too far.

"You said you might have a solution," Joe says gravely.

The tapeworm bobs back and forth happily. "I knew you'd come around. First thing you gotta do is get somebody's attention." It looks all around, then swivels and inches away, leaving a wet trail of slime on the tiles behind it. "This way."

Joe follows the worm back to the section of the locker room where he left his backpack. The worm reaches the bag first, and sticks its head into it, fishing through the contents of the bag with its teeth. "You got a lighter in here?" asks the worm.

Joe grabs the bag away from the worm, setting it on the bench. He reaches into one of the outer pockets and produces a Bic lighter, despite his misgivings. "What do you want a lighter for?" says Joe, though he has a feeling he already knows.

"We gonna light us a little signal fire," says the worm. "Empty out your bag."

Reluctantly, Joe upends the backpack onto the floor of the locker room—soiled clothes, a pair of sneakers with the soles worn through, an empty bag of Doritos, and a notebook filled with sketches from when Joe dreamed of being an artist. The worm seized on the notebook. "This'll do nicely. Light it up."

Joe opens the spiral notebook. The first pages are loose, unattached. They're the oldest drawings in the notebook, from when Joe was little. Some of them are even in crayon—his old house, his old dog, young Joe and Mommy and Daddy under a smiling yellow sun. He pages through the book briefly, a chronological tour of his art work. By high school he was doing high-contrast charcoal portraits, including a self-portrait. He looks down at it, into his own tired charcoal eyes. "This is mine," he says softly. "My art."

"Yeah, yeah, I know," Tommy says dismissively. "You been carrying that thing around since I met you. But let's face it, you never gonna *do* anything with it. It's just an anchor on ya now. An old dream you'd be better off forgetting. Besides, what else ya got that we could use for kindling?"

"Dad never wanted me to be an artist," Joe says, still flipping through the pages. "He wanted me to do a trade. Like… carpentry or something."

"Yeah, he's a douchebag," Tommy replies. "Can we get on with it now?"

With a sigh, Joe nods and drops the notebook on the floor. He watches with numb sadness as the worm nudges the notebook under the wooden bench, then opens the book and begins shredding pages with its sharp, circular mouth. It scatters the pages about, as if making a nest. Then it arranges Joe's old dirty clothes, draping them over the wooden bench just so. All the while the worm hums the chorus from "*School's Out*" by Alice Cooper.

As he watches, Joe's sadness crystalizes into anger. He's put up with so much from his father. It's his father's fault Joe's life is the way it is. His father's fault Joe never amounted to anything as an artist. In some ways, it's his father's fault Joe is an addict.

It's his father's fault Joe's trapped with Tommy in this awful white room.

"Hey, Joe," says Tommy. The worm gestures up at the ceiling. "Plug up those emergency sprinklers, will ya?"

Joe stands on the bench and pushes the little nozzle with the heel of his hand until it folds back flat against the ceiling.

"Ready when you are, champ," says Tommy, slithering back from the bench, where Joe's belongings have been artfully arranged to catch fire. Joe reaches under the bench, finds a strip of paper to start the fire. It's a sliver of his self-portrait, his eye and a piece of his mouth. Joe lights the end of it, shoves it back under the bench, and steps back.

Long tendrils of smoke wreathe up from the bench, and in a moment, Joe's soiled clothes catch flame. The nylon sleeping bag starts to melt into the wood. The smoke alarm high on the wall starts to ring and Joe clutches his ears, wincing at the piercing noise. The emergency sprinklers go off and drench Joe, but the one above the flame is bent and produces only a thin trickle. The fire grows under the bench.

Joe and Tommy move back, to the other end of the locker room, as black smoke begins to billow, filling the upper heights of the locker room like thick summer clouds. Joe gets down low, clutching his sweater over his mouth. Tommy is beside him.

"What do we do now?" cries Joe.

"You've got to hide!" says Tommy. "Come on, follow me."

The worm slithers back into the bathroom, and Tommy crawls after him. Tommy approaches the square grate of the ventilation outtake that Joe tried to break into earlier. Even as Joe watches, Tommy seems to *flatten*, and easily slips through the metal grate into the vent. The screws at the corner of the grate appear to unscrew themselves as Tommy turns them from the inside, and the grate crashes down from the wall. Inside the vent, Tommy waves at Joe with his tail.

Coughing and sputtering, Joe climbs into the big vent shaft, feet first. He pulls the grate back onto the wall behind him, and then crawls backward into the vent. The metal bangs and rattles as he crawls further into stuffy darkness. Everything smells vaguely of old gym socks.

The worm is somewhere in the pitch darkness behind him.

"That's enough," Tommy says, sounding amused as always.

"You don't want to back up into the fan, do you?"

Joe tries to catch his breath, but the smoke is being pulled into the vents. He can't get enough oxygen. "I can't breathe!" he gasps, trying to wriggle further back.

Tommy nips at his heels. "That's enough, I said!"

Then from the locker room comes the sound of a battering ram on the door. Joe is ecstatic, and starts to crawl back out of the vent. This time, Tommy bites down on his heel and doesn't let go, so that Joe cries out, kicking until the worm releases him.

"You stupid or something?" Tommy hisses. "Your father will have you arrested for arson if you're caught. Don't think he wouldn't!"

Joe nods, feeling lightheaded. His hands are throbbing and bloody from his previous struggles to open the door and the vent grate. Only his rage keeps him conscious and alert. He waits, biding his time and listening.

He hears the door to the locker room bang open, hears the masked voices of the firemen and the hiss of chemical fire extinguishers. He can see nothing but shadows moving against the lights through the grates of the vent. The firemen talk, men move in and out of the room.

Finally Joe hears *him*.

"What do you mean the place was empty?" His father's voice sounds high and shrill. "My son was in here."

"Looks like someone set the fire and ran off," says another voice. "Just a minor little thing, more smoke than fire. The benches are treated so they don't burn. We found this—"

"That's his backpack, damn it!" says Joe's father, the Dean.

"We're calling the police. We just wanted to notify you, sir—"

"Yes, do it!" cries the Dean. "Get out of here, all of you! *Get out!*"

Joe listens, waiting for the door to close. Then he inches closer through the vent, toward the grate. His father is just outside the vent, to his surprise. "There's blood on this grate," cries the Dean. "Idiots! Get—"

Joe thrusts the grate out, smacking his father in the face. The older man stumbles backward, stunned. His horn-rimmed glasses are cracked and he looks like a startled owl. "Joseph?" he cries. "What the hell?"

Joe flops out of the vent, glaring at his father. "You locked me in," says Joe, rising to his feet. "You locked me in here on purpose, you bastard!"

The Dean raises his hands. "Calm down! I didn't lock you in anywhere! The door here doesn't even lock. Now, son…"

"I'm so tired of your *bullshit!*" Joe shrieks. He shoves his father, and the older man loses his footing. The Dean falls backward, cracking the back of his head against one of the porcelain sink fixtures in the bathroom, leaving a smear of red. The old man looks up, dazed, and Joe pauses above him, his eyes fierce with hatred.

Tommy the tapeworm slithers in from the direction of the locker room. "Go ahead, Joe," he says cheerfully. "There's nobody here. This is how it has to be. You need your fix, and I need to feed on ya. He's gotten in the way for the last time."

The Dean reaches up feebly from where he lies between the sink fixtures. Blood drips from his fingers. "Joseph…" he whispers. "Please… I'm your father."

That only incites Joe's rage. He kicks the old man in the ribs. "You're no father of mine!" he cries. "You stupid bastard!" He kicks him again. "You were never there for me!" And again. "It's *your* fault I'm here!" And again. And again.

"This is how it has to be," Joe whispers, breathing hard. "You got in the way for the last time…"

He stands over his father.

The old man lies still beneath him, crumpled and beaten. His shattered glasses lay beside his blood-stained face. His white circle of hair is stained pink with blood. A slow horror creeps over Joe, and he feels sick to his stomach. He crouches, shaking the old man.

His father doesn't move.

"Dad," Joe whispers, his face stretched in fear. Tears spring unbidden from his eyes. "Dad, I'm sorry. I'm so sorry, Dad. Get up. Dad!"

Tommy slithers toward him. "Good work, buddy," he says.

"Now let's get out of here before someone finds him. We got things to do, you and I."

Joe whirls on the worm, his rage returning through the tears. "Shut up! This is your fault!"

The worm rolls its black, pig-like eyes. "It's always *someone else's* fault with you, ain't it?"

Joe lunges for the worm with a wordless roar, and it dances aside, leaving Joe to crash chin-first on the bathroom tile. Dazed, he looks up—and the worm is gone. He gets up, looking around nervously. The room is still acrid with the stink of burnt wood and plastic, and tendrils of smoke linger in the dark corners. Joe pads to the front of the locker room, back to the door.

He smacks into it shoulder-first—and bounces back, just as before. "No!" he screams, banging the door desperately. "Let me out! Somebody help! My dad's hurt!" He keeps banging on the door until his knuckles split and bleed, leaving red smears across the stainless steel.

Finally he slides down to his knees, sobbing quietly.

From the bathroom comes a gentle slurping sound. Joe hears it, swallows fearfully. He gets up and creeps back, leaning around the wall to look in the long narrow bathroom.

Under the sink, his father's body seems to be encased in a white sack from the chest down. The sack is pale and slimy and throbbing, slowly rising up the Dean's bloody suit jacket to encase his entire body. There are teeth at the top of the sack, opening and closing, slowly dragging the sack up the length of the Dean's body. Black and pig-like eyes shine up at Joe.

It takes Joe a moment to understand what he's seeing.

Tommy is eating Joe's father whole, like a snake.

By the time Joe understands, the worm has slurped its way up over the Dean's broken nose, his closed and twitching eyes, his bloody receding hairline. Joe screams out—and then his father is gone. The worm's mouth closes around the Dean's head, and Tommy grins at Joe, now huge and bloated.

"Thought I'd remove the evidence," says Tommy, his voice now deep, swollen as his body. He laughs, and the sound seems to shake the entire bathroom.

Joe takes a step back, not believing his eyes.

"What's wrong, Joe?" says Tommy, tilting his enormous white head, now the size of a mastiff's, and grinning. Blood drips from teeth sharp as knives. "I told you I was getting hungry. What's with all the attitude?" The voice seems to be growing deeper, more monstrous.

And the creature slithers closer.

Joe finally runs, screaming, out of the bathroom, back to the locker room, slamming against the door like an animal, banging and shrieking against it and losing his mind. The thing, the creature, slithers closer, its slow wet movements rasping through the smoggy room. Joe bangs his head against the door until it bleeds.

He keeps pushing the door, never noticing in his panic the small, faded sticker that says PULL.

A shadow falls over him as something slithers nearer, humming.

"Oh, Jo-seph," it says, in a singsong voice. "Where do you think you're going? I'm still so... hungry."

The Hunters

"I just want to make the kill already," says Leo, through a shiver. "All this waiting. It's always the worst part."

I sip my tea, lukewarm from the Sterno, and nod in silence. The two of us are squeezed into a high tree stand, at the end of a cold and fruitless hunting trip. I'm bundled in two layers of thick wool and thermal underclothes, with two pairs of wool socks and insulated rubber boots, and my toes are still numb. The waiting is bad, yes, but for me the cold is always worse, the way it settles in like an unwelcome guest.

Next to me, Leo frowns. "I never understood how you hunters can just sit here like this." His thick legs are shaking, from cold or restlessness or both. "I'd go crazy if I had to sit here by myself."

"You never done this in your line of work?" I ask. "What about a stake-out?"

Leo laughs, a gasp of grey fog in the night air. "In a warm car, with a donut and a Playboy, if the Mets ain't playing."

"You get used to it," I whisper. "It starts to feel... like you're part of nature. Part of the woods, the mountains. Like you belong here."

Leo says nothing. I eye him as I sip my tea. He looks like any other ex-cop I've ever met—big, maybe 240, with a round belly and a shining bald head. His goatee's gone grey, but no doubt was once as thick and black as his eyebrows. His heavy brow gives his eyes a hooded look, almost scowling, as if everything around him were suspect.

Up until this weekend, I'd never seen Leo in person. We met online recently through the Ronald Swanson League of America Game & Gun Club. I had been living in the cabin here on my cousin's hunting property all winter, recovering after a bitter divorce from the world's biggest slut. All winter, with only a slow dial-up line, the meager lights from the solar generator, my Mosin-Nagant rifle and the cold cathedral silence of the woods to chill the rage inside me, and the loneliness—the hollow loneliness like nothing I've ever known, so lonely it's not even a feeling but a lack of feeling, an empty place where something should have been.

So when Leo messaged me through the Game & Gun Club

forum, suggesting we share a little hunting trip, I was eager to accept his offer.

"It is better," I say, clearing my dry throat, "having some company for a change."

"I love you too." Leo's laugh turns into a dry emphysema cough into his mitten. "If only there was some shooting to go with all the love."

"Yeah, yeah."

I feel like I know Leo pretty well for someone I only met in person this weekend. You get to know a person pretty well after a few days together on a sixteen square foot deer stand. First just the usual things. I learned how Leo spent 25 years on the police force, first in New York, where he was shot in the lung in a drug raid, then here in Pennsylvania, where he finished out his years behind a desk without complaint. In turn, Leo learned about my failed farming career, my dabbles in taxidermy, landscaping, gas station attending. I heard about Leo's first wife's passing—cancer—and his second wife's hot little Latina body and the fact she's half his age. "And never talks back." Leo heard about my cheating whore of an ex-wife, how I found her with the neighbor, how she didn't even have the class to act embarrassed, how her overpriced lawyer still convinced a jury to give her custody and half my assets, which in practical terms meant our house, our cars, her damn engagement ring. Everything.

"You know," I tell him, "this land was once an ancient Indian burial ground."

After a while, you run out of stories about yourself, so you find other stories to tell. By now we'd gotten around to scary stories and urban legends.

Leo smirks. "Oh yeah?" He's fiddling with the CB radio, turning it over idly in his mittened hands.

"It's true, actually. Or at least that's what my uncle told us. We used to come up here when we were little, my brothers and me. I even came with the wife a few times. Bitch loved the Appalachian Trail. There's a gorge just over the border, in the state park. They say that's where Indians buried their loved ones."

"Wailing Gorge," says Leo. "Yeah, I know all about it."

"Wailing Gorge?" I repeat. I've never heard it called that.

"Near the Appalachian Trail? Where those bodies were found a few years ago?"

I grin, realizing Leo is spinning a new story to trump mine, almost as if he's had it at the ready, like a well-played hand of cards. Leo's poker face doesn't change—he looks at me from the corner of his eye, his face stone.

"It was all over the news. Some hiker stumbled on it, around 2000, 2002, but the bodies must've been there a long time, they were only bones and rotting clothes. Three bodies at the bottom of the gorge. One of them was butchered, hacked into little pieces. They say they never found all the pieces, and that's why you can hear a woman wailing down there sometimes. Still looking for lost body parts."

"That's just the wind," I say. I've been to the gorge before, plenty of times. There's no real boundary separating my cousin's land from the state-owned wilderness to the northwest. "Anyway, I was being serious."

"So am I," he says curtly. "All this really happened, Ben. It's on police record."

I don't remember hearing it before, but now that I have, a part of me thinks the tale sounds familiar. Had my uncle known about this? Tried to hide it from us?

Leo snorts, shakes his head, and says something I don't understand: "It's like this every time. You never remember. Or, rather, you only remember what you want to remember."

At that moment something catches my eye, a flash of movement out in the underbrush. I scramble to raise my rifle and put my eye to the scope. About thirty yards away, at the edge of the clearing, stands a doe, maybe a hundred pounds. I can hear Leo readying his own weapon. "There she is," I whisper. "Do you see her?"

The doe has stopped right in the middle of the path, her head turned away, looking at something to the north. I watch her ear twitching, surreally slow, my heart hammering.

"Hey, yeah, there she is," Leo whispers, his voice calm for a first-timer. "Finally."

"Take the shot," I urge. It's his, what he's been waiting for.

Then through my scope I see the deer bolting, scrambling into the brush.

"Shit," I start to say, "let it go—"

Then the sharp, echoing *bang* as Leo squeezes off a shot from his Springfield. "Got her!" he says. I scan the edge of the clearing with my scope, seeing nothing. "Did you see that?" boasts Leo. "Dropped her in her tracks!"

I put the rifles in the bucket winch and start to lower them as Leo unbuckles from his full-body safety harness and backs down the ladder. "She didn't get away?" I ask as I hurry after him, handing him his weapon and strapping my own over my shoulder. Our boots crackle over the dead leaves of winter.

"Yeah right," says Leo, grinning. He holds out his hand like a pistol. "Head shot, baby. Works every time."

I nod, laughing, feeling exhilarated. If the cold and the waiting are the worst parts, this is by far the best.

I stand in the middle of the path, looking around. There are hoof-prints where I last saw the doe, moving off at a run, but Leo ignores the tracks, stooping over the brush on the other side of the path. My gaze follows him, and my breath stops short. For a long moment I can only stare.

Partially concealed by the brown yew tree above, the body lies in a sprawled heap, twisted by the bullet's velocity, legs kinked up, arms splayed out to either side. Not a deer.

"Oh my god…"

A female hiker, her face completely ruined by the round from Leo's 30-06 Springfield, nothing left but exit wound, a sunken red bowl of brains and blood. The bullet took her from behind as she fled, through the center of the skull, the blood soaking her long blonde hair into thick and ugly clumps. She wears a dark brown jacket, a muted red cap. So surreal, like something on TV.

"Leo…" I murmur. "You… you…"

What have we done? What have we done? For it is *we*, him and I, I'm his guide, I'll be drawn up too—accessory charges—my poor cousin Jamie and my nephews, all dragged into it, hell, my ex-wife, the slut, and my poor sweet daughter, my life as I know it at an end.

I recoil, vomiting over my boots, chunks of Slim Jim and canned raviolis ugly as blown-out brains. "The radio," I manage through wheezing breaths. "Give me the radio. We have to... have to call somebody..."

Through my bleary eyes I see Leo staring at the body impassively, his face as blank as a sleepwalker's. Then he stoops and takes the body by the ankles and drags her out onto the path, her limp arms following grotesquely.

"What are you doing?" I cry, my fingers pressed into my temples. "We have to call it in. We have to tell the police."

Leo chuckles, shakes his head. "Yeah, I'm sure Judge Reiner would love to finally get *me* up on his stand. But nah, I don't think so, buddy. That ain't how this works." He tilts his head. "How about you help me out for a change?"

"*Help* you?"

"I thought not," Leo sighs. He bends back to the dead hiker, beginning to pull off her boots.

"What the hell are you *doing*? You're a cop—this is a goddamn *crime scene!*"

"I ain't been a cop in a long time, Ben," Leo says, in a bored tone, as if explaining something obvious to a child. He manages to wrench one of the boots away, sniffs inside it casually, tosses it over his shoulder.

I dodge the shoe as it bounces past me, then seize Leo by the shoulder. He stands at once, shrugging me back. The man towers over me, almost a hundred pounds bigger, eyes hooded black pools. "Stop it, Ben. Don't make this any harder than it has to be. We were just talking about the Gorge, for Chrissake, and you're still gonna play this game? That's where she's going, Ben, just like before. Just like always."

The body wouldn't be found for years down there, maybe decades, and meanwhile Leo would be in Costa Rica living it up on his pension. And me? I could get away too. I could get away...

Instead I unsling my Mosin-Nagant and level it at Leo point-blank. "Don't move!" I cry, but too late—Leo's brought up his own gun too, and suddenly I'm looking down a cold steel barrel myself.

"You can't do this," I say. "I can't let you. Just give me the radio, man."

He only smiles.

"Look, it won't be that bad," I plead. "It was an *accident.*"

"What are you waiting for, buddy?" Leo sneers. "Oh, Ben, Ben, Ben. If you were capable of pulling that trigger... I wouldn't be here now, would I?"

"Drop the gun and give me the radio. Now."

Instead Leo fires. My right leg folds in half beneath me and I topple backward even before the pain kicks in, the sharp and swelling great radiant pain. I look down at the blossoming red bullet hole in my thigh and start to scream, somehow getting my gun up and returning fire wildly, but Leo has already sank back into the brush. In shock, I push myself backward with my elbows and good leg, hugging my rifle at my chest.

Once under the cover of brush I strap my gun over my shoulder and roll over onto my belly so I can crawl away faster, wriggling into the deep evergreen briar thickets that snarl the edges of the path. I slide down a little hill, tumbling over and over, leaves spinning with me, like laundry, and at the bottom I splash to a stop in the cold muddy gulch and roll over to aim my rifle at the top of the ravine behind me. For what seems like hours I wait, shivering, the gun bobbing in my trembling hands, my breath hitching in and out.

When I'm satisfied he's not coming, I roll over and crawl down deeper along the little gully, just to be safe. The pain is unbearable now, throbbing out from my thigh in waves, my right pant leg soaked with red. At last I stop, wedged in the hollow of a great evergreen's roots, where I remove my belt with a wince, tighten it into a tourniquet above the inch-wide bullet hole in my thigh, where the hollow-point went in and out. My lucky day.

Just when you think you know somebody.

How long has it been since he shot me? Minutes? Hours? How long before I bleed out?

Suddenly I hear a giggle behind me and seize my gun, my heart in my throat. I lurch away from the tree, ready to fire. "Who's there?" I demand. But no one answers.

That wasn't Leo. That voice was female.

I rub a glove across my sweat-soaked brow and stare up at the trees, huge and alien above me. I'm feverish, I realize. The wound's been infected, or blood loss is bringing on delirium, or something. I have to get that CB radio. It's my only chance to leave these woods alive.

I roll over, and stumble to my feet, supporting myself on a nearby tree.

When I turn around, I come face to ruined face with the walking corpse of the hiker. There's nothing left above her lower jaw. Just the red remnants of her nasal cavity, a few broken teeth, and the sloping bowl of her empty brain-pan, the little entry hole visible at the back.

Something slips away inside me as I study her grinning jawbone, her ears, her lovely blonde hair streaked with crimson. I hear screaming, somewhere, my own, and next thing I know I'm running, scrambling from the ravine, hopping and skipping on my useless leg, tripping up in the woods and crawling on, wrenching my way back to my feet. I see it all as if from outside myself. Flopping clumsily into a prone position in the brush, scoping out the camp site: the deer stand, the sleeping bags below, the path leading away toward the Appalachian Trail. No sign of Leo. I look behind me, half-expecting to find the ghastly revenant of the girl in pursuit, but of course there's nothing.

Just the fever, I tell myself, trying to calm my breath. I'm seeing things.

When I cautiously approach the camp site, the woman's body is gone.

There are footprints all around where she fell. Some of them are Leo's heavy boot prints; others, smaller, appear to belong to the hiker. There is a trail of blood through the grass, other than my own, heading the quarter mile toward Wailing Gorge.

They could be anywhere. Stalking me from the trees. I could be in Leo's sights right now. Leo…

Or *her.*

Revenge she wants revenge I'd want revenge—but no, that wasn't real, just delirium, focus, *focus.* Leo. The radio.

Every step is a loud, lurching struggle, dragging my throbbing leg along like plywood, using the bare trunks of the evergreens for support. The blood trail is easy to follow, and besides, I know where it's headed.

I hear Leo long before I see him.

Leaning against a tree trunk, I peer around to watch him. Up ahead, Leo stands at the edge of the Wailing Gorge, humming merrily, his back bent over his work, sawing away at the dead hiker's arm-pit with a long serrated buck knife. As I watch, he severs the arm, and sets it aside next to the other quartered body parts in a neat little row. His rifle rests against a stone a few feet behind him. I don't see the radio anywhere.

I lurch out of the trees with a burst of adrenaline, holding him at gunpoint as he's flinging body parts over the cliffside. "Stop!" My voice hoarse and wild. "Stop, you bastard!" Leo pauses in mid-throw, holding half a leg in both hands, and looks over his shoulder at me, his breath misting.

"You're late," he says, and tosses the leg over the edge.

The wind howls out of the gorge behind him, womanish and shrill.

"You hear that?" he says, amused. "The echo of the past."

Never taking him out of my sights, I shamble in close enough to kick his rifle out into the gorge. "Hey!" Leo says, more indignant than angry. He starts to approach and I gesture threateningly with my own gun. "That wasn't necessary, was it?" he grunts, raising his hands. "Ain't this what we came here to do? To make a goddamned kill?"

"Not like this," I whisper. "Not a *woman*."

Leo shakes his head. "Not just *any* woman, Ben."

"What do you mean? You saying you knew her? Did you set this up?"

"Not me. *You* did. A long time ago. Maybe 2000, 2002? I don't remember. Guess I'm starting to lose some of my memories, too."

I've never looked insanity in the eyes before, but now I know— the dark, hooded gaze, the pig-like intelligence.

"Oh, Ben, Ben, Ben." Leo shakes his head, and sighs. "God, I've seen this show too many times. The regret, the confusion, the denial. I guess it's *my* punishment."

"Who the hell are you, really?" I demand. "You're no lawman."

"Uh-oh, he's getting warmer," Leo says over his shoulder, as if to the gorge, or the blood-stain where the girl had lain. "I *was* a lawman, till they benched me, put me in early retirement at my own desk. I had to take up other lines of work. By then I'd made certain... connections..."

"You're him, aren't you?" I say. "The killer. That story you told me, the bodies in the Gorge. That was you."

Leo laughs. "I prefer the term *hitman*, but you're so close! Come on, Ben. *Think.* Why are we here?"

"Shut up," I whisper, done. "Where's the radio? Give it to me."

"Here's a hint—take a look at that hand over there." Leo gestures with his head.

"Stop talking and give me the radio."

"You and your radio. Don't you know by now it wouldn't do us any good? Just take a look." He sneers. "Come on."

I glance in the direction he's gesturing. A few feet away from the bloody spot where he butchered her, the dead hiker's left hand remains, severed at the wrist, the last piece of her that hasn't been scattered to the bottom of the gorge. I'm reluctant to remove my eyes from Leo, but something makes me double-take. There's a ring on the dead hiker's finger. A diamond engagement band.

And suddenly I picture the hitchhiker—what was left of her—with a new recognition.

Her long, blonde hair.

Her white, soft skin.

"Oh, no," I whisper. "Oh, no, no no..."

"Go on and take a look," Leo is saying, his hands still raised, but I'm already moving closer, Leo half-forgotten, sinking to my knees in the pool of blood to stare at the hand. Tears have blinded my vision, but I don't need to see it any closer. I know that ring.

She used to wear it, even after the divorce. She kept it in the settlement—even that—and she loved to lord it over me.

"Starting to remember now?" Leo says. "This is usually where it comes back—"

I lunge to my feet, shoving the barrel of my rifle against Leo's chest. He stands nonchalantly, his hands still on his head, still wearing that careless smile. I can only sob for a moment, staring at him across the length of the gun. "I'm going to kill you," I tell him firmly. "No—you're going to do it yourself. Walk backward."

"What about your precious radio?" Leo mocks.

"Screw you!" I scream through the tears. "Walk backward. You're going in that gorge too, you piece of shit. Jump!" I drive him back with the rifle, my finger itching painfully over the trigger as I picture the beautiful stream of his guts flying out his back, but no. I want it to be *clean.* "Jump!"

At the precipice, he wavers on his heels, lowering his arms for balance. "Wait!" he shouts. "The radio."

I hesitate long enough for his hand to snake down to a pouch on his utility belt. He removes the radio slowly, holding it by the plastic handle, his eyes locked on mine. "Here," he says. "You'll need this."

"You killed her," I sob. "You killed my wife."

"It's what you hired me to do, pal," says Leo. "I told you not to come along. Told you to just call her, get her out here on some pretense, and let me handle the rest. If people like you could handle this stuff, the world wouldn't need people like me. I knew you wouldn't have the guts for it. If I'd only listened to my instincts, we'd still be alive today. Instead we get to play this out again, every night, for all eternity. The night we all died. Thanks to you and your sudden conscience. You and your *weakness*—"

Leo shoves my rifle aside, swinging the radio in the same instant, whamming me across the face hard enough to break the plastic. I stumble aside, falling on my gun, inches from my ex-wife's severed hand. Next thing I know Leo's on top of me, crushing me under his weight and grabbing for the rifle as I twist beneath him. The severed hand skitters away over the ledge in the chaos as we wrestle for control of the gun.

"This time I'll change it," says Leo, through gritted teeth. "This time—"

My finger presses the trigger and the blast rings in my ears like a bell and a chunk of Leo's shoulder seems to vanish; he falls off of me with a howl and I manage to crawl away, struggling to my feet at the edge of the gorge.

Leo crouches before me; and a few feet behind him, my ex-wife stands with her blown-out face, her lower jawbone seeming to grin.

Then Leo lunges for me, I fire the gun over his head, and he tackles me at the waist. Somehow I manage to grip him by his coat, pulling on him for leverage to keep from falling, and for a moment we teeter together on the brink. In that instant, Leo leers up at me, and I see the void, the emptiness behind his eyes, behind his smile.

"Till next time, Ben."

Then we go over together.

Somehow I cling to the side of the ravine, my fingers digging into rough dirt and stone, fingernails tearing away from the friction. Leo's fingers grip for purchase on my blood-slick pants, find nothing. Then he's gone. The wind howls in my ears as I cling there, shivering.

I look over, and there on a shelf of rock just below me rests my ex-wife's severed hand, the diamond ring glinting faintly in the gloom, as if alive with some inner light.

I try to reach for it, sobbing, telling her I'm sorry—for in this instant, all the memories come flashing back, and I understand what Leo meant. Too late, as always. Nothing ever changes. "I'm sorry, honey," I whisper through my tears, reaching for her severed hand. "I'm so sorry. I was wrong, God damn it. I was wrong! You didn't deserve this. No one deserves this."

If I could just reach the hand, maybe. If I could just get the hand and explain to her, maybe our fate will change. Maybe this will be the last time our restless, tired spirits have to play this out again.

As my fingers brush the ghostly pallid hand, my own grip slips on the muddy roots and instantly I plummet into the darkness of the rift, endlessly, a moment stretched into eternity, a moment of recognition, recognizing my guilt, knowing I will forget again tomorrow, knowing no amount of regret will change our fates.

My contrition has changed nothing.

As the wind wails past my ears, I hear her giggle.

The Accident

The burgundy Oldsmobile struggled down the empty wooded road, buffeted by the gale outside. The car was a late eighties model, almost as old as Ivan himself. It had always given him trouble, but never as much as tonight. The wipers did nothing against the onslaught of rain, and the headlights seemed to flicker, the light was so drowned out.

"Pick up the pace," Rodriquez complained beside him. Ivan's companion sat low in the passenger seat, his lanky legs folded, like a man on a park bench on a sunny day. As though they weren't hurtling in an ancient death-box through what seemed like a hurricane.

"I can't see shit," Ivan replied, clenching the wheel in a death grip.

Luckily, the road was empty. Most folks had places to be on a night like this, homes to occupy, dinners to eat, fireplaces out of the rain. All Ivan had was Rodriguez, and their mutual boss—an angry Bolivian drug lord back in New Mexico, waiting for the twenty thousand dollars Ivan and Rodriguez carried in the trunk.

"Castro gonna be pissed if we're late," said Rodriguez. He smirked behind his thick mustache and goatee. Idly his hand touched the grip of the pistol shoved in the waistband of his jeans. "You ain't gonna like Castro pissed."

Ivan ignored him. The surly old spic had been ruffling his feathers the whole trip. He seemed to take this job as an insult, babysitting Ivan on his first big east-coast run. Rodriguez thought he'd been sidelined because of his bad knee. Ivan thought he was probably right. He also thought Rodriguez was a bitter old asshole.

"Shut up and let me drive," Ivan said, leaning forward and squinting through the river running down the windshield.

Static started breaking up the formulaic pop song on the radio. The static increased in volume until it consumed the music altogether. Ivan frowned and turned the knob to a different station—but the sound did not change. He twisted the knob back and forth, full circle, slowly, quickly. Nothing. Every station was static.

Rodriguez started to shout something and Ivan glanced up just in time to see a great brown shape passing through the headlights as something leaped from the side of the road. He wrenched the wheel, too late, and with a heavy thud the brown thing smacked the hood, went up and over. Then the car was spinning, skidding on the slick gravel as Ivan frantically pumped the brake.

Finally the car stopped, and Ivan sat in the cab, dazed, listening to his heart hammering and the radio static and the steady tin drums of rain on the roof. Beside him, Rodriguez sat slumped over the dashboard. "Hey," Ivan said slowly, jostling the Mexican's shoulder. "You all right? Rodriguez?"

The man emitted a low groan, but did not move. His head was busted open above his thick unibrow, and blood dripped slowly over his folded up legs, down to the stained and dirty floor mat.

"Shit," Ivan swore.

The collision had killed the engine. Still in the dream-like daze of shock, he removed the key and got out to inspect the damage. The wind drove the rain in at an angle like hard cold bullets, drenching him instantly.

He hurried around the front of the car, now fanned out across the median line. An ugly, blood-smeared dent surrounded the shattered right headlight, deep and jagged as a canyon. Blood streaked up over the hood and across the right side of the windshield. He looked around for the animal he'd hit, but it must have been further back down the road, and he could barely see two feet in front of him.

"Stupid deer," he whispered, unaware that he was slowly, ceaselessly shaking his head. "Damn stupid deer." This was exactly what he didn't need. Like hitting the storm of the year wasn't bad enough, he had to hit a goddamn *deer*.

And where had this storm come from, anyway? It had been sunny when they left New York.

He got back in the car and cautiously tried the ignition. The engine revved when he turned the key, but refused to turn over. He tried again. Then again. The nervousness solidified in his belly into a hard, indigestible lump.

Out of nowhere, the static on the radio seemed to expand, a low, metallic rasp rising to a shrill crescendo. It was so horrendous to the ears that Ivan instantly punched the knob to turn off the radio—but the sound did not change. It wasn't coming from the radio, but from the speakers themselves—or from within his own head. It rose like an alarm, until he clutched his hands over his ears and screamed soundlessly into the noise—

Then, as suddenly as it began, the shrill static noise fell silent. The one remaining headlight went out and the wipers stopped in place, and suddenly the only sounds were the heavy rattle of rain and a dull ringing in Ivan's ears. He tried the ignition again, but the engine did not respond. The car—engine, battery and all—was suddenly dead altogether.

"Goddamn it!" He smacked the faux leather steering wheel with the heel of his hand.

He would have to call somebody, which he hated to do, with twenty thousand in drug money in his trunk. But what choice did he have? He could at least call Castro, let him know what was happening, so hopefully the bastard wouldn't kill Ivan's family if he was a little late.

He fished in his pocket for his cell phone, flipped it open.

The words 'No Signal' greeted him in flashing red.

He stared at it in shock. "No way," he said again. "You've got to be kidding me." He stared at the unconscious Mexican in the passenger seat beside him, as if for an answer. "What the hell do I do now?"

They'd passed a town a half-mile back—a little junction of two state highways, with some old houses built up to the roadside, two gas stations, a convenience store. It would be hell in this weather, but he could walk back there and find a phone. Castro would know what to do.

He shoved the Mexican back in the passenger chair so Ivan could access the glove compartment and the blue emergency kit, where he found the flashlight inside. The beam was dim and wavering—he hadn't changed the batteries in years. As he fiddled with the flashlight, he noticed the handgun shoved in the waistband of the Mexican's jeans. No sense leaving that unsupervised. He leaned over and pulled the gun free, tucking it in his own pants, behind his back and under his shirt.

He got out into the inch-high rain, put the car in neutral and rolled it off the road. Then he opened the trunk, stared down at the black knapsack inside. He wasn't about to leave twenty thousand sitting unsupervised, either. He'd really be dead if he lost *that*.

As he passed the site of the accident, he scanned the beam up and down the flooded asphalt, moved by a kind of curiosity to look for the deer he'd hit. He found only a trail of blood, so thick and black it was barely diluted by the pounding rain. The blood led away into the shivering woods beside the road. Whatever Ivan had hit was gone.

So the lucky bastard got away after all, at least for now. He doubted it would live for long. Ivan shone the light at the dark trees a moment. "Good work, asshole!" he shouted through the rain. "Hope you die nice and slow!"

His anger only grew as he made the long walk back toward the town. The rain bore down on him and the chill sunk deep into his bones. The wind literally moved him, swatting him about like a cat's plaything.

The terrifying moment of the accident kept playing through his mind. The sight of the brown animal, just a blur in his periphery vision as he looked up. The way it went up and over the hood, and the car spinning out of control.

Ivan couldn't believe his uncle Fyodor had once called deer

cunning. What the hell kind of idiot animal would be out in weather like this? No deer Ivan had ever heard of. He used to go hunting white-tail with Uncle Fyodor, before the dumb bastard got himself killed over some unpaid gambling debt.

With wind and rain this bad, most deer would bed down somewhere and wait it out. These conditions made it too hard for a prey animal to detect predators.

Could he have hit something else?

As he walked, Ivan thought about the first deer he'd shot. He was no great marksman—in fact, despite his newfound career in drug-running, he'd rarely held a gun aside from those hunting trips with his uncle—but that first deer! He'd shot it dead on, just behind the shoulder, piercing its vital organs in exactly the right way to bring it down clean. Beginner's luck, his uncle called it. He remembered how the buck kept stumbling for another thirty feet before seeming to realize it was dead, how its legs folded under it and it spilled down at last in a heap. He remembered the sight of it, up close, afterward. The black dead eyes, already crawling with flies.

Maybe this was karma, he thought, with a dark smirk. The deer's last revenge.

Something cracked in the woods beside him and he turned to see a great tree limb crash down into the road, mere feet in front of him. Branches lashed his face like whips. He stumbled back, blinking in the rain. Blood ran down his face.

He stood there a moment, breathing hard and cursing. Then he thought he saw something move out of the corner of his eyes. He turned, studying the woods. His dim flashlight caught a glint of something, like two shining embers—just a flash, and the eyes were gone.

Ivan swallowed, then convinced himself he was seeing things. He hurried around the fallen tree, moving down the road, scanning from side to side with the flashlight. Each step made him feel more panicked, until he broke into a jog. He kept looking over his shoulder. *He* felt like the prey, now, disoriented by the rain. The noise and torrent of the storm made him feel deafened, vulnerable. Yet he was certain he could hear something, under the noise. Something stalking him through the woods beside the road.

The town was dark at this hour, but the lights were still on in the convenience store just before the intersection. The warm glow of the store front emerged suddenly out of the gloom, like a lighthouse, before Ivan even realized he'd made it. Gasping, he sloshed the last few yards, through the empty parking lot to the glass doors, and staggered inside, the bells above chiming his entry.

"Hello?" he cried, as he came in. "I need help!"

But only silence answered. The clerk's desk at the back of the store was unattended. Receipts and empty cigarette wrappers had blown to the floor, scattering like autumn leaves as the wind blew in behind Ivan.

He stood there, his heart still hammering as he looked around. The whole store was only five short rows of shelves, packed with bread, doughnuts, Cheetos—the necessities. Milk and soda chilled in cold storage along the back wall. There was no one in sight.

He walked down the aisles, pausing at the medicine section and grabbing a Band-Aid. He pushed back his dripping hair and felt his forehead with his fingertips. The bruised cut from the fallen tree limb was just above his right eyebrow. He laid the Band-Aid over it, then wiped the blood from his fingers on a roll of gauze.

Thunder bellowed, a beast outside the rattling glass doors. Ivan was glad now he'd chosen to make for the town, as the storm was only getting worse. He could feel himself growing calmer, now, the panic and irrational fears of just moments ago fading like a dream.

When he turned around, a young man stood behind him, and Ivan nearly leapt out of his skin. "Jesus!"

The young man adjusted a bundle of merchandise under his arm, giving Ivan a look of scrutiny. He was younger than Ivan—perhaps sixteen or seventeen—with very short black hair and a piercing through his nostril. He shrugged. "You all right, bro?" he said in a low voice.

"You always make habit of sneaking?" Ivan demanded. In his surprise, some of his parents' Ukrainian accent crept back into his voice. "Do you work here? I'll pay for the bandage..."

"Nah, man, take it easy." The teenager shrugged toward the empty desk. "It's Old Tom's shop, but I don't know where he is." He narrowed his blue eyes, which Ivan suspected were surrounded in eye shadow. "You're not gonna rat on me, are you?"

Ivan glanced at the merchandise tucked under the young man's arm—a two liter of Coke, a box of Twinkies, magazines, condoms, and cigarettes. "What are you, *looting*?"

The boy looked around incredulously. "I don't see anyone I could *pay*, do you? I just got stuck here. I been here twenty minutes, man. I saw *you* steal that Band-Aid."

Ivan adjusted his heavy backpack with a shrug and a small smile. As if a little criminal activity meant anything to him! He turned and walked toward the clerk's desk. The young man watched him warily, and asked again, "You all right, man? You not from around here, are you?"

"My car broke down," said Ivan. "Where's the phone?"

"Behind the desk," said the boy. "But I already tried. It's dead. Same as my cell." Ivan discovered the phone beside the register even as the young man spoke, and held the receiver to his ear. Silence. He stared back at the boy and the boy said, "You have to wait it out, man. This place must be on a generator or something, cuz the power in my parents' house went out already. Want a Twinkie?"

Ivan slammed down the receiver. "Can anyone in this shit hole fix a car?"

"Yeah," said the boy, sardonically. "Old Tom could."

Ivan cursed under his breath. "So this guy just up and leaves, doesn't lock up the store or anything? Where the hell is he?"

"He lives upstairs," the young man replied. "I called up, but no one answered."

Shivering and irritable, Ivan went to the corner, beside the cold storage, to the old rusted door labeled "Management Only". When he touched the handle, the door opened with a creak, revealing a staircase to the second floor.

"Hello?" Ivan called. His voice bounced back from the dark, narrow stairwell. He thought he heard something up there, like a voice on a television or radio. He took his flashlight from the mesh pocket on the side of his backpack and turned it on. The beam flickered on and off, no matter how he shook or hit the torch. Hesitantly, he began to climb the stairs, calling again, "Hello? Uh... Old Tom?"

"Hey, man, don't call him that to his face!" the boy whispered behind him.

Thunder struck again like a bombing run, shaking the building. The door at the top of the stairs rattled on its hinges, and creaked open as if to welcome them.

Ivan stood on the landing and peeked through the door, scanning the room beyond with the flickering flashlight. The small apartment was dark and empty. In one corner stood a kitchenette—an oven, a fridge, a sink. Nearby, papers and store receipts littered a small breakfast table. A television buzzed, displaying static, the only pallid light in the room. A gun rack was mounted above the television, but there was no gun to be found.

A short hallway led off from the living room, and down that were two doors. Ivan could hear a radio from that direction, and one of the doors was open a crack.

"Hello!" Ivan called irritably, coming into the apartment. "Hey, I want to pay for this Band-Aid…"

No one answered. Ivan crept down the hallway, toward the radio broadcast, which—like the one in his car—was intermittent with static. Occasionally a voice broke through.

"…frequency clear… repeat…"

Ivan pushed open the bedroom door. There was no one inside. The bed was unmade. Clothes and belongings were strewn about the floor. Either the old man was a slob or he'd been packing things in a hurry. On the nightstand, the radio struggled to play.

"…Frequency clear… Repeat…" said the broadcast, harsh with static. "…From the sky… no civilians on the streets… safer indoors… repeat… sightings…" The voice sounded further away with every word that broke through. "…repeat—" Then the voice cut out altogether.

From the doorway behind Ivan, the boy said, "That sounded like Rebel 88. They broadcast from a tower right down the road. Can't believe it's coming in so bad."

Ivan adjusted the volume knob on the radio, but the voice was gone in the static and noise, too distant to discern. "They were talking about sightings."

"Sightings? Of what?" said the boy.

"Maybe a tornado?" said Ivan. "How should I know?"

"They said something about *from the sky*, didn't they?" said the boy, smirking. "Maybe it's an alien invasion?"

"Maybe hail," Ivan said irritably. "Do you see a computer? I really need—"

At that moment, a thunderclap shook the building, closer than ever, and lightning flashed through the room. Suddenly the radio static went silent, as well as the air conditioning, and Ivan realized the power had gone out.

"And there goes the generator," said the boy, almost cheerfully. He seemed to be enjoying this. It was probably the most exciting thing that ever happened in a town like this.

Ivan muttered a curse in his native tongue and shook his head. So much for a computer. The storm was getting worse every minute, and after that weather report—or whatever it was—the conditions seemed even more dangerous. "Let's go back downstairs," he said. "Maybe safer there."

He left the empty bedroom and crossed the apartment. But when he reached the landing of the staircase, he heard something that made him halt.

Downstairs, the bells above the front door chimed as someone came into the store.

"That must be Old Tom," said the boy, sounding a little relieved. "Let's go tell him we're here."

But Ivan grabbed the boy's shoulder. "Wait," he whispered. A sudden sense of fear had gripped him, and at the same time he remembered his flight here through the rain, how certain he'd been that something pursued him in the dark.

The boy raised an eyebrow as Ivan passed him. Reluctantly, Ivan crept down the stairs, easing his wet sneakers down onto each wooden step, nervous of making a sound. Down below, the door out to the store was open a crack. He turned off his flashlight, stood there and listened.

He could hear it moving through the store—something *big*, disturbing merchandise on the shelves as it passed. He could hear it dragging itself across the floor with a slow, rhythmic rasp of flesh on linoleum. He could hear its shambling, broken gait; one leg dragging, another leg clicking like a cowboy boot—or a cloven hoof. He thought he heard breathing, too—heavy, wet and rattling.

Ivan listened behind the door, unsure what he was hearing. Part of him wanted to call out to the visitor in hopes of hearing a human voice in response. But fear held him mute.

The stairs creaked behind Ivan and he turned to find the boy inching down behind him. "What is it?" he whispered.

Ivan gestured sharply for the boy to shut up. Then he listened.

There was only silence in the store, now. Whatever was in there was listening back.

In his mind, Ivan saw the thick line of black blood on the pavement, tracing the movements of the creature as it dragged itself, lurching and heaving, out of the road, into the forest, to nurse its wounds and its malice. Ivan tried to remember the shape that had jumped across the road. Hadn't it been too big for a deer? Too big—and too dark?

What had he hit out there?

He turned and ushered the boy back up the stairs. The boy had heard the strange movements as well, and when Ivan's bouncing torch light caught his eyes, they were wide and white. "What the hell is that?" he demanded. His voice was little more than a tiny exhalation, but even that seemed loud now in the darkness.

"Shh, shut up," Ivan hissed urgently. This idiot was going to give him away unless he did something. "Go hide," he whispered. "Go hide and shut up."

The young man backed away, into the bedroom, and eased the door closed behind him. Meanwhile Ivan drew the gun from his waistband and looked around the living room of the shopkeeper's apartment. There seemed to be nowhere to lay an ambush. A flash of lightning painted the fogged round windows white, and suddenly he lost his resolve. He crept backward, opened the bedroom door, and joined the boy in hiding.

The boy peeked up from the other side of the bed. "What the hell am I hiding from?" he whispered. Then he saw the gun in Ivan's hand and sank back, staring at it like it was something from another planet.

Ivan barely noticed. He set the flashlight down on the dusty dresser so he could run a hand through his damp, dark hair. He couldn't catch his breath. "I don't know," he whispered. "I don't know. I hit something with my car. I hit something and I think it followed me here."

The boy swallowed visibly. "What was it?"

"I don't know," said Ivan.

"The radio mentioned *sightings*," said the boy. "And something *from the sky*. What was it you hit?" When Ivan didn't respond, the boy continued: "Was it something... normal?"

"It must've been an animal," Ivan insisted. "It must've been. A deer or something."

"Maybe that's where Old Tom went," the boy said miserably. "He must've seen something, or something got to him."

"Shut up!" Ivan hissed. He leaned against the wall, looking out through the cracked bedroom door into the rest of the apartment, too dark to see. He could just make out the door to the staircase.

The door was still ajar. And he could hear the stairs creaking, slowly creaking, as something made its way up toward the apartment.

"Shit," Ivan whispered, his knees feeling weak. He eased the bedroom door closed and locked it, then crept backward until his back was to the dresser. "Shit."

"What do we do?" the boy cried, too loud, starting to panic.

Ivan raised his handgun and leveled it at the boy across the bed, who froze and gaped at it in wide-eyed terror. "*Shut. Up*," Ivan hissed.

Out in the living room, the apartment door banged open. The visitor was inside with them now.

Ivan could hear it shuffling through the living room, as if inspecting every corner. He heard a chair fall over, heard a low grunting sound, and a hoarse rattling breath. Whatever it was, its gait no longer seemed so slow and broken. It seemed quick and frantic, now, eager to meet the new playmates hiding up here.

The gun was shaking in Ivan's hand as he held it on the staring boy. He wasn't about to die like this, to whatever monster was outside that door. He was going to walk out of here no matter what it took.

"Get up," Ivan whispered. "Get up." He motioned the terrified boy toward the door with the gun. The boy rose like a zombie, holding his hands above his head, his eyes never leaving the long barrel of the .38 Smith and Wesson revolver. His pants were stained with urine.

"Hold the door," Ivan commanded. He leaned back and ripped the curtains from the window behind the nightstand, and fumbled to open the window with his free hand. It was locked, or stuck. Meanwhile he tried not to let the boy out of his sights. The boy leaned against the bedroom door, starting to sob now and mutter some prayer.

And suddenly a devastating weight crashed against the door, rattling the cheap hollow door in its frame. The impact bounced the boy back, and he cried out in terror as he fell back against the door, holding it down. The impact came again, and Ivan heard the door frame splinter and the boy was sobbing.

"Oh please God I don't want to die. Oh please—"

Ivan held the gun on the boy. "Hold that Goddamn door!" Then he turned and smashed out the window with the butt of his gun. The wind wailed inside like a banshee, throwing back the curtains and drenching Ivan in rain. He kept smashing out the glass until it was all gone and the plastic interior frames broke away and the bottom of his hand was shredded and bloody, then he leaned out.

There was nothing outside the window—no roof, no gutter, no ledge, no tree to grab hold of, just slick and moldy vinyl siding and a dizzying fifteen foot fall to the dumpsters below.

He looked back at the boy. The boy had his whole back and arms pressed against the door, his legs braced in front of him. Behind him the door buckled and splintered. A fissure opened down the center of the wood. Something in the darkness beyond was growling and snuffling, a sound not of this world.

The boy stared back at Ivan. His blue eyes were wide with knowing terror.

Under a final blow, the door shattered beside the boy's head, and the boy fell aside. The door came free of its hinges and began to open.

Ivan didn't wait to see what would come in. He turned and dove through the window, the boy's scream ringing in his ears.

The dumpster below rose to meet him.

He landed in the mound of black bags with a thud, and screamed out instantly in pain. He clutched at the side of his thigh, where a long piece of broken glass had pierced through a trash bag, his jeans, and an inch of his flesh. Blood dripped out steadily, hot on his hands. He wrenched the glass free and gasped at the jolt of pain.

He dragged himself to the edge of the dumpster and half-jumped, half-fell over the side, into the asphalt, where he lay wincing and bleeding. The wind seemed to press him down to the ground and tug at his soaked clothing. Through the torrent, he couldn't see the window from which he'd jumped, nor could he tell—was the boy still screaming inside? Or was it only the wail of the wind?

When he tried to lurch to his feet, he cried out and collapsed again, wincing. He'd twisted his ankle, too, maybe broken it. He tried again, and managed to stumble across the parking lot, tumbling down a gentle hill into an overgrown ravine. He got up and kept running, the gun still clutched in his hand. He had no idea where he was going.

Then he saw something blinking in the sky up ahead, and at first thought it was an illusion—or, God forbid, a spaceship. Then he remembered something the young man had said, about a local radio tower.

If they could broadcast a signal, maybe they could get him help.

He limped toward the blinking red light, through an empty lot behind the convenience store until he found himself walking alongside the road. He thought he saw rundown old houses passing by on his left, but the lights were out there, too. He could barely see two feet in front of him. Only now did it occur to him that he no longer had his flashlight—nor the backpack with Castro's drug money. He'd lost both in the dumpster, and he wasn't about to go back now.

"Hello!" he screamed at the top of his lungs, praying there was someone still alive in one of the houses. "Hello? Is anyone there? Hello!"

The answer came from behind him—a sharp banging sound and then a rattle, like a can kicked into the street. Ivan whirled, swinging his gun back behind him, but he could see nothing. He felt isolated, imprisoned in a cell of water and darkness, while the grinning, slavering warden could be anywhere in the night beyond.

Ivan turned and ran as quickly as he could, clutching his bleeding leg with his free hand. "Hello!" he shouted at the dark houses. "Anyone! Hello? Help me! Oh, Christ, anyone?"

But there was no answer. He was alone.

Another sound behind him, like the clink of broken glass under a heavy foot.

Not *quite* alone.

He ran as if Hell itself chased his heels, heedless now of the pain. His sneakers pounded the slick asphalt of the highway's shoulder, but however fast he ran he was sure if he looked back the thing would be there, snarling, opening its jaws for his throat.

The radio tower was just ahead, through a small thatch of woods. Ivan left the road and plunged into the trees. Branches and thicket lashed at him like groping arms. Terrified, he ran on, swatting at the invisible tendrils that poked and grabbed him, feeling through the utter darkness on desperation and instinct.

The rustling noise of his own passage nearly deafened him to all other movements, but faintly he heard the pursuit, crashing through the trees behind him, scraping bark in its passage and churning leaves in its wake.

The woods broke suddenly and he was on the last field between himself and the radio tower. It was up ahead, atop a gentle slope. The lights in the little building underneath were on.

Ivan went on, his breath coming in ragged gasps. The slope, which would have been nothing in good weather, had turned to a rainy mud-hill. He was halfway to the station when his feet slipped. He screamed in pain as his ankle turned beneath him again and spilled him down to the mud. Immediately he rolled over, pulled up the gun, ready to fire at whatever was coming up fast—

But there was nothing there. He squinted bleary-eyed through the darkness, searching all around him. Not a damn thing.

"Jesus," he whispered. Could he have imagined the whole thing after all?

He turned back to the radio tower.

And something big was standing there in the dark.

He screamed out, raised his gun, and almost fired. Only at the last moment did he stop himself.

It was Rodriguez, the Mexican. His partner, whom he'd left unconscious in the car. The big man stood there in the rain, looking at him in a kind of daze. Ivan couldn't believe it.

"Oh, thank God," he gasped. "It's you."

But the Mexican said nothing, only continued staring at him. Then, slowly, he took a shambling step closer. In the gloom, his face looked blank. Ivan couldn't see his eyes. He thought he was muttering something.

"Rodriguez?" Ivan took a step back. "You all right? Hey, I didn't mean to leave you back there. I just—"

Without warning, Rodriguez lunged the last yard between them, tackling Ivan to the ground. Suddenly the Mexican was wrestling Ivan for the handgun, elbowing him and prying at his fingers. "The hell?" Ivan grunted, beneath him. "Get off me!"

"The money," the Mexican was mumbling. "Stole it."

"I didn't steal anything!" Ivan squealed. "I went to get help! Rodriguez!"

But the Mexican's big hands were strong as a vice, and Ivan couldn't get the gun away from him or get himself out from under him. He kept wriggling and struggling, trying to get away—and suddenly he heard a tremendous bang, ringing in his ears, and all the fight went out of him. The Mexican got the gun away and rolled over, leaving Ivan stunned in the mud. He looked down at the fresh blood running from the gunshot wound in his jeans, a baseball-sized hole in his thigh.

"Jesus Christ," he cried. "You shot me!"

Rodriguez looked over at him, his jaw hanging slack, like a zombie. The bloody contusion on his head looked swollen as a ripe melon. "You stole the money," he said slowly.

"I didn't steal anything, asshole!" Ivan shouted. "I took the money with me to keep it safe. You think I could've left twenty grand sitting in a trunk? What if somebody'd found you sitting there?"

Rodriguez studied him a moment with dull incomprehension.

"Where is it then?" he slurred finally.

"I dropped it in the dumpster," Ivan grunted, clutching his thigh. As the shock wore away, the pain was coming in fierce and bright. He could feel himself getting weaker, floating away from his body. "It's in a dumpster, back by the store. God, you shot me, *kurva blyat!* You shot me real bad."

The sight of Ivan bleeding out seemed to wake Rodriguez from his stupor a bit. "Sorry," he said. He gestured loosely at his head. "Think I got a concussion or something. I don't feel right, *ese.*"

"Fucking asshole!"

"What should I do?" Rodriguez said, with an almost child-like innocence.

"Just get me to the radio station," Ivan gasped.

Rodriguez leaned over stiffly and dragged Ivan like a sack of potatoes, paying little heed when Ivan screamed out in pain and clutched his bleeding thigh. They found the door of the station slightly ajar. Inside, they came to a small lobby, empty. A wall separated the studio, which was visible through a glass window. Like the convenience store, it was empty, and the lights were off inside, save for a few tiny orange emergency lights.

Rodriguez dragged Ivan into the studio, leaving a long trail of blood over the tough industrial carpet. "What should I do?" Rodriguez asked again.

Ivan looked around, his eyes bleary from the pain. The radio's control deck was as confusing to him as a pilot's cockpit. Still, he recognized the hanging microphone above the DJ's empty seat. He gestured to it feebly. "Call for help," he said. "Anybody. Just get somebody out here."

Rodriguez tapped the microphone. There was no indication of any sound. He started looking around the console, pushing buttons. Meanwhile Ivan clumsily undid his belt and wrapped it around his upper thigh, pulling it into a tourniquet above his wounds, so tight he cringed. Then he sat there, his head leaning against the console, focused on not passing out. He suspected if he lost consciousness now he would never wake.

"I don't know, man," said the Mexican, scratching the back of his head. "I can't figure it out. I think something's wrong with the power grid. We're on auxiliary, man."

"God, it hurts," Ivan grunted, clutching his thigh. He laughed raggedly. "I was thinking, for a while there, it was the end of the world. I thought I was being chased by something... unnatural." He ran a hand over his face, which was drenched with sweat. "I was kinda hoping it *was* the end of the world. Seems like it would improve the status quo, you know?"

Rodriguez squatted beside him. Overhead, thunder shook the radio tower. "Don't talk," said the Mexican.

Ivan ignored him. "I was never cut out for this business," he grunted. "I should've stayed in the old country. Land of opportunity, they called it. What opportunity? Work in McDonalds, scrub out toilets? And then comes Castro, with his big fancy car, and his girls, and his bling. What a salesman, that guy, eh?"

"Now look at me," he went on. "Bleeding out from a gunshot wound. After holding a damn kid hostage so I can jump out a window." He paused, looking up at Rodriguez. "That *was* you back at the store, wasn't it?"

Rodriguez only stared at him blankly. "What store?" he said.

Ivan sat upright, despite the pain. "The convenience store," he said. "Did you let the boy go?"

"What... boy?" Rodriguez repeated. He was staring in a distracted way through the glass window at the front of the studio, out into the dark lobby, as if he saw something out there.

Ivan stared at him. "No," he said. "No, no, you're kidding, right? I thought I was being chased by a goddamn space monster or something. But that was *you* in the store, it had to be. God damn it, don't joke about this. Rodriguez?"

But his partner no longer paid him any attention. The Mexican stood in a slack-jawed daze, much the way he'd looked when Ivan first encountered him. "I feel... strange..." he murmured, in a slurred voice. He was still holding the gun, which twitched in his hand.

As Ivan stared at him, something else caught his eye. He'd just noticed an old rotary phone on the wall across the room. "Rodriguez," he said. "The phone." But his partner ignored him. Ivan wondered how badly he'd hit his head.

"Do you hear that?" Rodriguez said.

Ivan rolled over, wincing, and started dragging himself toward the phone across the room. His leg felt almost numb. An icy chill had settled deep into his bones. He suspected he had little time left. Yet he managed to reach the phone, scrabbling up the wall to reach it, and holding it to his ear.

To his amazement, he heard a dial-tone. It was like sweet music.

He dialed 911, and waited as the number rang. His smile faded when a recording picked up.

"We're sorry. All operators are unavailable due to call volume. Your call cannot be connected at this time. Please hold for an operator to assist."

And then 911 played elevator music.

"Ivan," said Rodriguez again, his voice dreamy. "Do you hear that?"

"Hear what?" Ivan murmured, in a dreamy state himself.

Then Rodriguez doubled up in pain, and in the next instant Ivan was struck by it too—the same shrill sound he'd heard earlier on his car radio, the sound that hit him as his car died. Only now there was no question—the sound was ringing in his own head.

Then the orange auxiliary lights went out, and the high windows in the studio shattered all at once, like in a sonic boom. Brilliant lights flashed from outside, blinding. The first flash was white lightning, but after that the light came in colors—blue, red, yellow, green—blinking rapidly, splashing the studio like a scene from a rave. It seemed to pour in from every window at once. And the *sound* kept getting louder, more incapacitating.

"What the hell is that?" Rodriguez screamed over the roaring noise. He stood at the broken window to the station lobby, pointing his gun and staring at something in the other room. "What the hell is that thing?"

Unmistakable at this proximity, even over the noise, came a familiar growl from the shattered station door—deep, guttural, too big for any terrestrial creature. It sounded almost bovine, but long and slow, as if the pitch had been altered by a voice modulator.

Then the shrill engine-noise droned out everything, and Ivan cringed as it shook inside his head. It was as if someone had plugged invisible earphones into his ears. The sound became so all-encompassing he began to hear music emerging out of the noise. Like Beethoven's *Ode to Joy* by a full orchestra between his ears.

He saw the flash of the gun muzzle in the Mexican's hands, but the deafening gun blasts were drowned out. In the flashing strobe-lights he saw the Mexican's horrified face as he emptied his clip, stumbling backward and screaming wordlessly.

Then something came through the door at the front of the studio—a hulking shadow, moving fast and jerky in the strobe-light, like something from an old silent movie. It looked like a massive dog that had been turned inside out and burned black. Ivan caught only a glimpse of it in a flash of light—the wet black flesh, the long curved horns, the brutal bared fangs, open wide and slavering.

In the blaring silence of the noise, the monster pounced on Rodriguez like a tiger and brought him down behind the radio console. Ivan rolled over and scrambled across the studio, breathing in ragged gasps. He wriggled his way into a recording booth, pulled his limp and bloodless legs in behind him, like he was folding himself into a suitcase, and slammed the sound-proof glass door. He saw the gun flashing several times. Then, a moment later, Rodriguez crawled out from behind the recording booth, his dark face strained in terror. He crawled across the floor toward Ivan, and Ivan saw that Rodriguez's arm had been torn away at the elbow, leaving only stringy strands of red.

Rodriguez slammed on the sound-proof glass doors, screaming soundlessly at Ivan, his terrified face splashed with his own blood. Then, a moment later, something loomed behind Rodriguez and yanked him away, like a dog pulling on a chew toy. The Mexican's pistol fell to the floor outside the recording booth.

Not knowing what else to do, Ivan opened the door just a crack, enough to grab the pistol. He checked the clip. His Uncle Fyodor had shown him all about guns, while hunting deer, and suddenly all that forgotten knowledge came back clear as day. He had three shots left.

The emergency sprinklers had come on in the studio and through the mists he could hardly see a thing—then suddenly a cord of human intestine slapped the sound proof glass, dripping down with long slimy tendrils.

Red eyes flashed in the gloom, and the creature stalked toward the sound booth, emerging from the fog. Ivan didn't wait for it to get close. He remembered how his uncle had shown him, where the vital organs were in the chest cavity—and as the beast drew nearer, he lined up the shot at the center of the great broad creature.

He squeezed the trigger and the glass shattered outward. He couldn't see whether the bullet landed, but the creature paused, as if stung—then came on again, faster now, lowering its horned head to ram him.

Next thing he knew the glass was shattering *inward* as the beast put its jaws through the recording booth door, slavering and snapping and straining mindlessly to reach him. The demon's breath was hot and stank of blood, and he could see bits of Rodriguez between its two-inch teeth.

Ivan pressed himself to the back of the booth and fired his second shot into the gaping maw. At point-blank range, it was impossible to miss. The muzzle flashed between the creature's teeth and the bullet tore outward through the top of its skull with a splash of blood across the glass.

If the creature made a sound, Ivan couldn't hear it over the alien symphony in his head. The creature seemed taken aback, appearing to shake its head and splutter for a split second, almost as if it had to sneeze. Then it lunged in again, the broken glass pressing deep into the flesh of its thick, bullish neck. Suddenly the snapping jaws were an inch from Ivan's face, growing closer each time they closed. Cracks fissured through the glass as it gave beneath the pressure.

Ivan almost squeezed off his final shot—but it would do no good. Hitting this creature with his car had been no accident, he knew that now. It hadn't been lunging across the road—it had been lunging for *him*. In those final gnashing moments, Ivan realized this was inevitable. He was right before.

This was the way the world ends.

Not with a whimper, but a *bang*.

Ivan lifted his head and put the gun to his own chin.

At the last moment, as he squeezed the trigger, he saw the great loudspeaker hanging from the front of the booth, suspended from the ceiling by a steel cable. He didn't think. It was sheer instinct, like the first time he'd shot a deer. He aimed the gun, and fired.

The bullet struck the cable with a spark and the massive loudspeaker fell like a cartoon anvil, too fast for reality—one moment hanging in the air, the next coming down on the creature outside the booth with crushing gravity. The creature's head snapped backward and blood sprayed the glass of the booth.

The jaws kept gnashing, but feebly, growing no closer. The creature was unable to advance, pinned beneath several hundred pounds of audio equipment with its neck wedged into the jagged glass. Finally it lay there, panting, blood dribbling from its teeth.

Ivan lay there weeping in the darkness, and after a moment he realized he could hear himself weeping again. The horrific sound in his head had diminished. The radio station was now dark and silent. Only the ringing in his ears persisted, a fading coda.

A moment later the creature went still. A great purple tongue lolled out of its mouth.

Hyperventilating, Ivan pushed against the recording booth door, trying to free himself, but it was held closed by the vast dead weight of the monster coming halfway through the glass. Finally he used the butt of his gun and smashed out the rest of the glass, then dragged himself out past the stinking horned creature, ignoring the jagged glass ripping his clothes and slashing him open. He barely felt it.

In the pitch blackness, he made his way across the radio station, dragging his wounded legs. The floor was splashed with gore, warm chunks and wetness and the cloying stink of blood, all that remained of his partner Rodriguez.

He sat there in the silence and darkness, weeping softly, too stunned for anything else.

For a moment, the effort to keep going seemed far too great. Only the sudden thought of his family—his sweet new wife and newborn daughter in New Mexico, his old sick father and wise-cracking mother back in Ukraine—made Ivan stir. He had to get the money back to Castro to keep them safe. He had to see them one last time.

Ivan sat there, breathing heavily in the gloom. Then he started crawling toward the door.

He was halfway there when he heard a low, bovine groan from the recording booth behind him.

His eyes widened in terror. No, God, no. How could the monster still be alive?

Scrambling now in spite of the pain, he crawled through the broken glass doors at the front of the studio and out into the flooded parking lot. The rain was so heavy on the ground he could barely keep his head above water.

He kept picturing his family. In the final delirium of blood loss, it was all that kept him going. Not fear of his own death, but fear of losing them.

Everything he'd done, he'd done for them.

In slow agony he dragged himself through the woods, reaching one hand forward, then another. His legs were cold and numb as wood behind him. Distantly he thought he heard sirens.

As he reached the edge of the woods, he could see lights flashing through the trees, and realized he was seeing cars speed past on a highway. He tumbled down a little ditch, and suddenly he was there on the side of the road, watching camouflaged trucks fly past in the rain. They were already passing as he dragged himself into the road.

"Hey!" he screamed hoarsely, lifting himself on his knees in the flooded road and waving both arms at the fading motorcade. "No, wait! Please!"

Only at the last moment did he see the blooming lights as a straggling car came up fast behind him.

He had just enough time to turn toward the oncoming headlights, to see his life in flashes before his eyes as the engine bore down with thunderous noise. Just enough time to throw himself aside, too late. The truck didn't even slow down.

And then, the accident.

The Migraine

The guy with the glass eye dropped me off in Breezewood, the self-proclaimed traveler's oasis—a neon thicket of gas stations, derelict motels, and varicolored fast food joints crowded along a stretch of US 30 that connects a gap in Interstate 70. "All the interstate traffic has to pass through Breezewood to get on the turnpike and continue west," the one-eyed guy told me. "You'll have no problem finding your next ride here."

Five hours later, I was beginning to wonder if that was the guy's idea of a joke. It seemed *impossible* to get a ride. There were no roadside shoulders, no room for cars to pull over. Asking around at the local diner earned an invitation to leave the premises, or else. Even the truckers at the truck-stop drove past with helpless shrugs. For a hitchhiker, Breezewood was no "oasis"—it was quicksand, and I was stuck.

As the sun began to set, I resigned myself to spending the night there. I chose one of several motels boasting the cheapest rates in town. A cute Indian girl in the front office gave me a room key, a brochure of local attractions, and a funny look when I explained I wouldn't need a space in the parking lot.

The motel room was typical, right down to the underpowered air-conditioner and the vaguely offensive odor that I couldn't quite identify. In one corner sat a rickety coffee table, a small refrigerator in 70's brown-and-yellow, and a writing desk acting as a stand for the television; against the back wall, a tidy double bed. The lamp on the nightstand cast a thin glow through its dusty amber shade.

I locked the door, closed the window blinds, and then sat to peel off my clothes. My socks were pasted to my feet by blood and open blisters. I limped into the cramped bathroom; under tepid shower water, I used complimentary soap to slough away the grime of blood and sweat and asphalt, and felt much better for it.

Afterward I lay in bed, naked to the waist, and allowed myself a smile. It had been hard so far, this journey, but I was doing it; I was really *doing* it! I felt free and strong for the first time in my life.

I reached over and took a photograph from the pocket of my shirt, which was airing out on the bedpost. The photo showed my destination: an old, brown ranch on dusty Arizona badlands, encased in a broken-down fence. A small sign out front read *Welcome Home*.

The Homestead. A place for self-proclaimed mystics, mutants, and other misfits. People like me.

As I stared at the photo, I noticed spots of color floating across my vision. I blinked and they were gone. Probably nothing, I told myself. Probably imagined it. And if I felt a little dizzy, well, what of it? Probably all the car-exhaust from the day's travel.

I ought to get some rest, I decided; tomorrow I would find some way out of Breezewood, and my long journey to Arizona would continue. I turned out the light, crawled under the blankets, and flicked through the TV stations until I found something familiar—one of the *Poltergeist* movies—then turned the volume low. The white noise and blue light of a TV set often helped me sleep.

But even after such an exhausting day, sleep did not come easily, and I ended up watching the movie. After a while I had to squint; it was getting harder to see. Blind spots and swirling colors grew at the corners of my eyes, and now I knew with grim certainty that I wasn't imagining these visual disturbances.

A migraine was coming on.

I started to get nervous. I had hoped to reach the Homestead before one struck. Could I deal with it on my own? Without Dr. Redford's pills? The self-confidence I'd felt just moments ago was slipping from my grasp.

I got up while I still could and filled a cup of water at the sink. Water was the only weapon I had. Water, and my mind. Everyone said I had a powerful mind.

The pressure was already building above my right eye.

I set the water on the nightstand and eased myself into bed. I probed my temple and winced; the vein there was fat and throbbing. I turned away from the TV's glow and closed my eyes. Colors danced behind my eyelids.

If I could just get to sleep quickly enough, I could escape the pain before it began...

"You can't get away," someone said on the television. *"I've got you! I've got you!"*

I turned away—and even the pain of that small movement struck me stunned, whimpering. *Too late, it's starting, it...* It felt like someone had driven the nozzle of a tire pump into my brain and was steadily, gleefully inflating. I remembered how the doctors back in the ward had called mine the *blitzkrieg of migraines.*

Nausea came in a hot wave. I held a groan behind clenched teeth. Sweat dribbled from my brow; my own fear-stink was cloying and awful. I tried to focus on something, *anything*—on the shallow rhythm of my pallid rib cage or the movie droning across the room—

"Don't be afraid. We won't harm you. We love you..."

—which my blurry eyes could no longer define, while a buzzing whine drilled between my ears and the bed-frame creaked under the strain of my writhing.

The phone. There was a phone on the nightstand. One call to 911...

No, they'd find out who you are—they'd send you back to Redford's ward and—and by God, who cares, *if it'll end this—!*

Bracing myself for the agony of moving, I stretched my arm across miles of rumpled bedspread toward the nightstand. My hand hovered over the phone; but I couldn't do it. I couldn't call and risk my freedom. I lifted my glass of water instead, spilled some down my throat, the rest down my chin and on the motel comforter.

I leaned back against the pillows; my whole head felt heavy with pain.

Mind over matter, remember; focus, focus.

But this was too much. Tears fell freely from my swollen eyes. Shuddering, I leaned over the cup cradled in my hands, and a globe of dark sweat fell from my forehead into the water, exploded there into strings of red. I clutched a hand to my pulsing brow; it came away smeared with blood.

The water spilled over my thighs as I lurched from the bed, slouched to the bathroom, digging my fingertips into my temples, leaning against the wall, looking in the mirror—

Above my eyes, a vertical fissure was shuddering open, spurting blood down my forehead in streams. I screamed and the mirror shattered outward and I lurched away, leaving dark fingerprints on the grungy white sink basin.

My skull is opening up.

Blind, sobbing, I stumbled from the bathroom. My groping hand knocked the phone to the floor and I fell on the receiver, dialed three numbers, and lay there weeping, "Help me. Help me. My skull is opening up and it hurts so much. Oh, please, God help me..." After a while I was aware of someone soothing me on the other end, but I could not make out the words over the pain.

I remembered the risk all too late. *Now you've done it. Now they'll find you, take you back to the white room, back to Redford and the needles...*

Blood dribbled into my eyes and stung like liquid fire. I started to slip into unconsciousness, but even in that warm dark I was not spared the pain; I was laid naked to it.

In the dreams that broke up the darkness, faces visited me; people I had known: all the wardens, both the kind and cruel; the cold, stately nurses; the over-eager students who were the only strangers in the ward where I had lived all my life...

And finally Dr. Redford himself appeared, frowning down and rubbing his mustache. I floated up toward him, then away, through the shattered bay windows at the front of the motel room; a spotlight blinded me from above; the stark night was hideous with police lights. Redford walked beside me. He was arguing with someone...

"...*Too unstable for the chopper...*"

Something in my head went *blink*—

And I was strapped down in an ambulance, thrashing against the buckles of the stretcher, frothing like an animal; a woman was screaming; the overhead light flickered in and out; medical supplies flew from the open cabinets; orderlies held me down, trying to insert their needles—

Blink.

Someone was crying. The overhead bulb was dead; a dim emergency flashlight lay on the floor of the ambulance, shining a washed-out spotlight on the rear doors, splashed in blood. Dr. Redford slumped in the corner, clutching a cross.

Blink…

Dr. Redford's face filled my vision, all mustache and intense blue eyes. There was a bandage around his balding scalp. As I woke, he leaned back. I saw he was holding my photo of the Homestead.

The pain had receded to a dull throb at the front of my skull. Now everything was quiet. The engine of the ambulance was dead. The only movement was the rhythmic slap of the wipers outside the blood-caked rear windows.

"You found me fast," I croaked.

Redford was unsurprised by my waking. "Oh, Jimmy, I would have found you before morning, even if you hadn't called 911. Your radio waves are impossible to miss." He shook his head. "Very clever, though, palming your pills. But I fear you've done more ill than good. How'd you get the silly idea to run away? I should have never let you watch that television…"

"Wasn't the TV. The internet. I found out about… others like me… They went to… to…"

Smirking under his mustache, Redford held up the photo. "This place? The Homestead?" His voice was gently patronizing. "Home for psychics, psychos, and other supernatural flunkies, yes?"

"People like me."

He tore the photo in half and let the pieces fall. "There are no people like you," he said. "You're something else altogether."

"What happened to me? My head was…" I tried to touch my forehead, and found I was still strapped to the stretcher.

"You killed them all," Redford announced. His eyes looked dull, expressionless. He looked around the blood-streaked ambulance. "The nurse, the orderlies, the driver. You shorted out the engine and the radio. We went off the road—"

"*What happened to my head?*" I demanded, refusing to listen.

"The incubation stage is coming to an end."

Blink.

"You've never heard of Project Agatha." It was not a question. Redford was on the other side of the ambulance, now, looking over his shoulder at me. "Thirty years ago, an organism was found frozen in a three thousand-year-old geological stratum…"

My mouth tasted of metallic blood. Ghosts of color swirled at the end of my tunnel vision. The migraine was starting to return; my jaw tightened as if with the turning of a screw.

"…hollow bones and wing structures, increased cranial capacity, lack of secondary sexual characteristics—though she sported a reproductive system identical to a mature female *sapiens*. Indeed, despite her bizarre physiology, mitochondrial DNA suggested she was almost human. *Homo sapiens icarius*, she was called, jokingly. We named her Seraph.

"Perhaps most bizarre of all was her evident resilience. When they uncovered her from the ice, she was still alive. Sort of.

"She was in what they call a persistent vegetative state; her body was still alive, but her mind… her mind was long dead. At least, that's what we thought."

Blink—in a flash I saw a cherubic thing suspended in a blue tube of oxygen, her eyes like wells of ink.

"What living animal could be buried in ice for millennia and still draw breath? She was an impossibility. People feared her. A Frenchman involved in her excavation called her *le dormeur impérissable*: literally, the undying sleeper."

Redford was leaning down over me. Everything stank of gasoline.

"What did you do?" I whispered.

"We kept her alive—though I think she'd rather have died. She made her hatred for us well known: lowering the temperature in her room to below freezing, short-circuiting thousands of dollars' worth of equipment, driving men mad with visions. Even unconscious, she could still reach out…"

Nausea prodded in my belly. "She was psychic, then."

"Oh, yes. Truly the most fascinating discovery in anthropology." Bitterness spiced Redford's voice. "Not that anyone ever knew. The more we learned, the more classified Project Seraph became.

"The potential in Seraph's super-human traits had the feds

watering at the mouth. Increasingly our objectives shifted toward replication... breeding..."

"*Breeding?*" It was a struggle to hold in my vomit.

"I was against it! A lot of us were." He shook his head. "But what could we do? We knew too much. I remember a guy named Joe Douglass, tried to abandon the project. Called it all *a one-way ticket to Hell.* He put in his resignation, and forty-eight hours later he was a missing person, never to be found again. That's the way it was. We didn't have a choice."

I didn't want to hear any more. "What's that smell?" I demanded.

Redford ignored me. Tears stood out in his brown eyes. "They told us she was as good as dead—just a vessel to be used for our experiments. But how could any of us believe that, when we could feel her presence, her pain, her *anger,* like a rank smell in the room?"

He scrubbed his old, old eyes with the heel of his hand. "But it was for the greater good. For the advancement of science, the human species, the United States of America. They promised us millions in research stipends, comfort and success for the rest of our lives. So we went through with it. Extracted an egg, fertilized it, returned it to her womb. The child was born in eight and a half months..."

Pain throbbed a tense rhythm in my temples. I knew how all this added up, but I didn't want to believe it: "Please don't say that child was me."

"No," said Redford. "The first embryo aborted, in a matter of days. You were the ninth, and the only one to live past age four."

I vomited a little in my mouth, unable to turn my head, coughing and spluttering it out from my lips.

"You see why you are unique?" Redford asked. Tears streamed down his sallow cheeks. "You are the heir to a whole new species."

I didn't want to believe. My whole body locked up as if to shield itself from the very notion. My head rang on and on, but I no longer cared.

"The *icarius* organism died birthing her twelfth child. After that, the science team was dissolved, its members reassigned. I was commissioned to care for you. You were raised under surveillance—"

"Please, stop…"

"We controlled your physical and psychic growth with medication. The military had certain specifications for how their 'super soldier' ought to grow up. They've long been waiting for a chance to get you off the anti-telegens, let you reach your full potential, but the risks…"

"*Shut up!*" I screamed, and the stretcher rattled and bent beneath me.

"Shh," he said, leaning over me, his grin nervous and frantic. "Don't you understand? I'm trying to tell you, I won't do it. I won't go through with it. I've seen what you can do. I won't let them release you on the world."

Panting, I squinted at him through the pain. "What do you mean?"

He stood beside me and brandished a medical scalpel. "Remember when I said the incubation phase was over?" he asked. "We've been holding it in check with drugs back at Detrick, but now that you've run off, you're going to enter the metamorphosis. Unless I stop it… manually."

He lowered the knife toward my forehead as I screamed in protest, placing the tip against my skull while I squirmed—but I was strapped in at the forehead, shoulders, elbows, wrists. I tried to reach out with my mind, the way Redford trained me, all those tests with the random number generators and sensory deprivation tanks and ESP cards with strange symbols. But I was stymied. I felt groggy, stupid. They'd tranquilized me.

"No," I whispered. "Please, no."

"Don't worry," the scientist replied, with a tired smile. "This won't kill you. But it will hurt. Very badly. I'm about to perform a minor frontal lobotomy."

"What?" I shrieked.

"Your headaches will be cured forever," he assured me. "And you'll be of no further interest to the military. You'll be free, like you want. Trust me, you don't want what they have in store for you. After the operation, there might be… other personality changes." He cleared his throat. "But we don't have much choice, here, do we?"

I strained myself psychically, pushing out with all my will, and Redford laughed sadly, as if he knew. "By the way," he said, "I wouldn't try anything while I'm trying to operate." He reached down with his free hand and pulled up an open lantern from his belt. "I've doused the whole place in gasoline. If I go down, this candle goes with me, and... boom."

"You don't have to do this," I whispered. "Let me go to the Homestead. Tell them I overpowered you."

"They'll find you," he said. "If you were allowed to mature into your full potential, you'd be a new generation of the atom bomb. A nuclear deterrent. A walking weapon of mass destruction. After... the things I've done... I won't have any more deaths on my conscience." He lowered the lantern back to his belt, then the knife. Then he reached beneath the stretcher and next thing I knew he was shoving a wooden gag into my mouth, tying it down. "There, now, that's better," he said, in soothing tones, as I grunted indignantly against the wooden bit. "You just bite down on that and close your eyes. Like I said, this is going to hurt."

He lowered the scalpel to my forehead, and I screamed.

Blink.

—grinding the knife on bone slowly coring out the skull and the sound is somewhat like dragging a fork across a ceramic plate, or fingernails down a chalkboard and the blood is spraying like a fountain down my face and shirt and pooling in my eyes to blind me and the pain is born, the pain is here, the gestation is over and the pain is being born on the end of a knife—

Blink.

"Almost there. Stay with me, boy—"

Now the ground was rumbling, and I could hear the distinctive weighty buzz of helicopters in the air above the wreckage of the ambulance. Someone on a loudspeaker spoke outside, and through the pain and the grinding of the doctor's frenzied scalpel I could just make out the words:

"Give him up, Redford. We're coming in."

Redford stumbled back from the stretcher, toward the back doors of the crooked ambulance, the blade in his hand dripping thick red blood. "Don't do anything stupid!" he roared, in a hoarse voice. "This whole car's soaked with gasoline and don't think I won't light it up!"

Through the pain my bleary eyes focused on the candle, burning in the lantern at Redford's belt. With all my will, I focused on the flame. A new sensation filled my head, a sort of cool, numb painlessness, and the flame flickered.

Redford turned around and stared at me, his eyes widening. "Oh, God," he whispered. "I'm too late." He dropped the scalpel to the debris-ridden floor and fumbled at his belt for the lantern, pulled it away, raised his hand to throw it down—

There was one final *blink* in my head, and when I came back from the blackness the ambulance was red, engulfed in flames. I was on the floor now, still strapped into the stretcher, which had collapsed. Redford burned beside me, his flesh slowly sloughing away. I felt the flames running up my own legs, heard the sizzle and crack of my flesh like burning bacon as if from far away.

Next thing I knew a flash-bang erupted the world in white blind light, and the double doors at the back of the ambulance blew open. Men in army fatigues and full-body hazmat suits appeared in a fog of fire extinguisher foam, and suddenly my stretcher was dragged from the furnace-heat and I felt a blast of cool air and saw the night sky up above through the smoke and then I was blasted with cold foam, smothered by heavy fire blankets. The night was alive with shouting and the drone of motor vehicles and helicopters.

"We got him!" someone shouted beside me. I could feel my stretcher being carried away while I suffocated beneath the wool blanket, breathing in the fumes of my own smoking body. "I need 90 cc of anti-telegens, 40 cc benzodiazapene, stat!"

Distantly I felt the needles penetrate my arm. The sensation felt far away. *I* felt far away. My awareness was no longer limited by time or space. I was awake. The world had opened in my mind and I was soaring over all.

I could see the hospital ward where I grew up, somewhere in the underground complex under Fort Detrick. At the same time, I could see the Homestead, the destination I would never reach, two thousand miles away. I saw it as clearly as if I were there, watching the wind blow dust over the desert plains in front of the old wooden cabin.

I saw my past stretched out behind me, and the threads of potential futures before me—what the military had in store: the systematic brainwashing, the sophisticated mind-control devices, rendering me a slave, a *machine*.

Then the war-fields, the snow-capped mountains of Russia, the sands of Iran, Syria, Pakistan, the rice paddies of Korea, China, Japan, all stained with blood and strewn with bodies at my feet. I see the bullets flying, the bombs and missiles tearing up the sky. I see myself walk calmly through it all, my head shielded and alien beneath an opaque helmet, the tanks and legions following, the enemies screaming, exploding, a million faces torn apart.

Redford was right. What they had in store for me was worse than anything. Redford only wanted to kill my mind. These men would kill my soul.

Someone pulled away the fire blanket and the military men looked down at me behind thick sunglasses. I could feel their fear as they carried me off on the stretcher, could hear every thought behind their hidden eyes.

"Morning, sunshine," said a voice behind me. A military colonel with a face like leather and a white beard and ponytail leaned over me. "Well, would you look at that! Fully transformed. You look just like your mother." He barked a laugh. "A shame we had to trick you into trying to escape just to finally force the transformation. Sometimes the science teams need an extra push, you know? Civilians! Am I right?"

This came as no surprise to me. There are no more surprises for me. Only inevitability.

"You're going to be a hero, kid, you know that?" said the colonel. "A God damn superhero."

"Yes," I said sadly. "I know."

This answer seemed to surprise the old colonel, and he narrowed his eyes. Meanwhile I could feel the anti-telegens and tranquilizers coursing through my veins; could actually pinpoint where the chemicals were en route to my brain and heart. I didn't have much time.

"Thanks to you," the colonel said in conclusion, "the world will fear America again."

I closed my eyes and allowed my mind to drift away, while I still could. Just like Dr. Redford taught me. I drifted up and up, to the helicopter circling slowly above. I slipped into the skin of the pilot, as easily as a man putting on clothes, and subtly I went to work on his motor coordination. As the pilot began to seize up, the helicopter drifted and the co-pilot started shouting. The helicopter spun in slow circles, tilting over, careening down toward the ground. Through the eyes of the pilot I could see the colonel and the other soldiers standing over me on the stretcher, shouting, looking up, too late. In the final instants I see the whites of my own two eyes, rolled back in my skull where I lay on the stretcher. And in my forehead, bulging and swollen with purple veins, my new third eye stares out from the fissure in my skull where Redford tried to carve it out.

In that instant I am aware of all things, a kind of blissful nirvana just before the end. I see the devastation that my own death prevents on a panoramic scale. In the final instant, as I drive the helicopter crashing into my own third eye, I see that the colonel is right, but for all the wrong reasons.

I am a God damn superhero.

And then I'm gone.

Sold As Is

"Honey! The toilet's doing it again!"

That's my mom, shouting down at Dad from the upstairs bathroom of our fifteen hundred square foot colonial. Mom's been cleaning the bathroom all day—or trying to. She and Dad are both stressed. It's tough selling a house nowadays.

One like ours especially.

"*Honey!* The *toilet!*"

One acre. Three beds, two and a half baths, wood fireplace and finished basement. Marble tile and Jacuzzi tub in master bath, new granite countertops and stainless steel appliances in kitchen. Dad's contractors really overhauled this old cottage, and the real estate ad with its flowery description and twenty photos catches every detail.

Every detail, but one.

"Oh, *God*, Frank," Mom wails, "It's *bubbling over!*"

"Coming!" Dad yells. His feet pound up the finished hardwood stairs. I hear Mom in the bathroom dry-heaving violently. I pad out into the hallway in my jammies, holding our kitten Rocko tight under my arm, my heart beating like that Energizer Bunny's drum. Holding a mop and bucket, Dad waves me back with a wide-eyed glare as he reaches the top landing. "Stay in your room, Lizzy."

He intercepts Mom at the bathroom door, hugging her as she sobs against him. I creep closer, hugging Rocko against my chest, until I can see into the bathroom for myself.

The toilet seat is rattling up and down as the toilet belches and burps underneath, and something thick and phlegmy and red bubbles out from the sides, pooling darkly in the crevices of bone-white tile. The lights above the sink buzz and flicker. On the mosaic shower tiles, words have been smeared in the same dripping fluid:

GET   OUT

And Dad wades in with the mop and a grimace, passing Mom's bloody sock-prints on the linoleum. "Get some towels!" he shouts, his voice hoarse and rattling from weeks of shouting.

Still hugging the kitten, I retreat backward to my room at the end of the hallway. My bedroom door is gone; Dad took it down when it started slamming shut on its own and trapping me inside. I sit at the foot of my bed and press my face in Rocko's warm fur, listening to his soft purr.

See, our house isn't like the others.

Our ad says *Sold AS IS* because some things no renovation can repair.

Sold AS IS was all the warning Dad got when *he* bought this place, in foreclosure, for what had been a bargain price, last year. Now he's *underwater on the mortgage*, whatever that means—I always picture him clinging to some mortgage papers in a crashing wave's tunnel, like a surfer wiping out—and we can't get out without a *short sale*, a silly name since it's taking forever. Nobody makes any offers, and the few offers we do get, from TV ghost hunters or demonologists looking for research subjects, the bank won't let us accept.

Dad is swearing in the bathroom down the hall, cursing God and hell and the devil in his rasping broken voice. This has all hit Daddy hardest. Mom says he feels guilty, or should, since he brought us here in the first place.

The light in the closet by my bed turns on suddenly by itself, shining cool and fluorescent through the slats, and I freeze. With a slow, stiff nonchalance, I rise from my bed and leave the room. The bedroom light flicks off behind me.

Rocko starts struggling in my arms and I put him down. Mom is standing in the narrow hallway, still crying and hugging herself.

"I think it wants to talk to me," I tell her.

She falls to her knees and holds me fiercely, pressing my face in her soft blonde hair. "No, baby," she whispers. "Please don't."

"It's in my closet again," I say, pointing back. "Maybe... if we just listened to it..."

"Stop it, Elizabeth!" Mom shakes my shoulders, her voice more pleading than firm, as if trying to convince herself: "There *is* no Walter, do you understand? There *is* no Walter!"

Yet—after my suggestion—the gurgling in the bathroom falls silent, and with it Dad's swears. A moment later Dad looks out at us from the bathroom, blinking, his white dress-shirt soaked with red blood. "Well," he announces, with hateful cheer, removing his blood-smeared glasses and wiping them with toilet paper, "that was even worse than last time, huh?"

"Walter said he'd make it worse," I reply. "Worse and worse, until we go away."

"Well *screw you*, Walter!" Dad exclaims cheerfully, waving jazz-fingers at the empty, neutral-paint walls. "Here's an idea! Why not start a gas-fire and *burn* this shithole *to the ground?*"

"Oh, God, Frank," Mom whispers, still squeezing me and rocking gently. "Can't we go back to the motel—can't we please God just *go?*"

Dad says nothing, replacing his glasses.

"You shouldn't have paid the mortgage," Mom moans. "We could've got a motel room… or bus tickets, plane fare... anywhere but here."

"And then what, Nadine?" Dad scowls. "The savings, the money from the move, it's all *gone*. If we don't get out with a sale, *we are toast*. You want me to just leave everything, leave the house, leave my job—like I'll just waltz into a new one?"

"Leave *what* job?" Mom snaps, releasing me and glaring back at Dad.

"Oh, that's rich," Dad says, with a rough and gravelly laugh. His smile is demented, smeared with blood like clown's paint.

The whole house seems to shudder.

"Please, don't fight," I try to interrupt. "It hates fighting."

But my small voice is ignored. Dad goes on shouting: "You think I *asked* to be moved ten states from home? Uprooted from everything, everyone, just to get *furloughed* a month later?"

"What about Lizzy?" Mom cries, caressing my cheek, looking at me with mist-filmed eyes. "We can't keep her here another minute. Think about your daughter."

"I *am*, Nadine. About the *consequences*, something *you* never consider! She'll make a real cute panhandler when we're *bankrupt* and Section 8!"

"Frank, stop," Mom whispers, still squeezing me and rocking gently.

"No, *you* stop, Nadine." Dad scowls down at her. "You think this is helping? Or do you even think at all anymore under all that Xanax?"

Mom looks as if she's been slapped and spins toward him, putting me aside. "Like you can talk, you *drunk*!" she screams.

Something moves in the attic overhead with a sound like claws skittering on the floorboards, like a rat, but much bigger.

Mom and Dad don't notice. Mom is fleeing downstairs and Dad pursues, shouting from the upper landing, "Wasn't your *sister* supposed to come get her? Whatever happened to that?"

"So now it's her fault?" Mom shouts back from the living room.

"Who the hell else do we know within two hundred miles!" Dad bellows.

The footsteps cross the attic space overhead again at a furious pace, *tap tap tap*. A family photo on the wall tilts on its nail, and dust shakes from the ceiling. The whole house seems to hum underfoot, like the tension in a bowstring.

I turn to look back at my bedroom. The only light inside comes from the closet, casting a slatted glow on the far wall. Downstairs Mom and Dad go on screaming and fighting, as usual. I approach my room reluctantly.

If I talk to it again, maybe it will leave us alone.

The disturbances began just a few weeks after the contractors finished and we settled in. Doors we left open would be closed when we returned. Objects slid off shelves without warning. The stairs began to creak late at night, starting at the bottom and rising toward the upper floor, while I shivered under my blankets, too petrified to look out into the hall. Every night the footsteps seemed to draw closer to my bedroom before they stopped. At first Dad would hear none of it. He blamed the contractors, faulty construction, quirks of a century-old foundation.

Finally one night, when the footsteps stopped outside my open door, I lowered my bed sheets and looked.

I've seen it several times since then, in several other forms—but none so awful as that first glimpse, before it knew to hide its true face. There was nothing recognizable, no human semblance, and I mistook it for something utterly alien, with its bulbous head void of features, its bony limbs and protruding ribs and black scaly skin like leather.

When I blinked it was beside my bed, looking in my eyes with empty sockets, milky with pus, set in black and fissured jigsaw flesh.

"*Get out,*" it whispered.

Only as it reached up languidly and caressed my cheek with a cold dead finger did I begin to scream.

After that things moved fast. The counselors, the hypnotists, the psychologists and parapsychologists, the psychics and priests and police, every one with a different explanation, a different spin. Meanwhile the disturbances grew more frequent, always at night, with no visitors as witnesses. Doors slammed shut when someone passed. Mirrors cracked as you looked in them. Small, strange footprints appeared in the snow outside the porch.

When we brought our kitten Rocko home, he seemed uneasy, spooked by the slightest noise, hissing at empty air.

Things seemed to vanish when you needed them most. Dad's papers and bills and late fee notices. Mom's deviled eggs before a PTA picnic. My homework.

All the features our realty listing doesn't mention. Sometimes light bulbs shatter in their sockets. Candles wink out in a wind no one feels. Flashlight batteries dwindle and go dead, brand new. There are no more footsteps outside my bedroom at night—instead I hear movements in the attic overhead, floorboards groaning as something seems to pace, endlessly, in circles.

I can hear those subtle movements presently, as I return to my bedroom. The temperature in the room is now twenty degrees colder. Frost clouds the window at the back of the room. As I enter, the fluorescent light from my closet wavers, then returns with a buzz.

"I just want to talk," I whisper. My voice is raw as red meat.

I stand two feet from the closet, the back of my knees pressed to my neat and unused bed, trying to discern through the glowing slats whether something is waiting beyond the closet doors. My heart sounds hideously loud, feels heavy in my chest. Downstairs Mom and Dad are still shouting, Mom telling Dad a short sale will look no better on his credit, Dad insisting it will but only if he *keeps making payments.*

"So says Carlos!" Mom shouts. I can hear her storming through the living room, then slamming the liquor cabinet shut. "And if you could trust a realtor, we wouldn't be here!"

Swallowing my trepidation, I move closer to the closet, and delicately slide one of the folding doors aside.

Something *bangs* within and I leap back with a yelp. The narrow stairs to the attic have fallen down on their own, filling all the closet. The fluorescent light is buzzing and flickering like a strobe. The long cord to the light switch is swaying, as if something has only just brushed past. My breath mists before me as I stare up the staircase into the gloom of the attic.

"Why won't you call a goddamn lawyer?" Mom screams downstairs. "I'm telling you, this was fraud! They... they failed to disclose!"

"Disclose *what*, exactly?" shouts Dad. "Disclose what?" Mom says nothing, and Dad's voice turns gloating. "Disclose what, Nadine? So suddenly you're a believer? Or should I say, *finally*! No more *group hallucinations*, no more drugs in the water?"

"We wouldn't even *be* here if it weren't for you!" Mom's shriek is punctuated by a scuffling sound and the shatter of a bottle, then Dad's shrieking curses and thuds of furniture moving and Mom weeping. The sounds make me feel like holding my ears and I realize I'm crying too. The tears feel like ice on my cheeks.

The walls of my bedroom seem to be breathing—*pulsing*, like the innards of a monster.

If I can convince Walter to leave us in peace, maybe it's not too late to save my family.

I step into the closet, the light still flashing intermittently. Not trusting the small and flimsy stairs, I creep up slowly on all fours, and carefully, carefully, peek over the landing into the dark attic.

At the back is an old filmy window, semi-opaque to the blue moonlight from beyond. A thin fog seems to enshroud the long triangular space, from the plywood floorboards to the pointed ceiling, and the attic seems vast as a result, infinite, ethereal. I pan my head all around. There's a rocking chair in the corner behind me. Boxes stacked to the side of the room, unopened since our move. Piles of furniture left behind by the previous owners—tattered sofas and burnt throw rugs and pewter lamps with torn lampshades, blanketed with dust. Antenna cables dangle from the pointed apex of the ceiling. Elsewhere, insulation hangs pink and exposed.

Dad's contractors never touched the attic—the one tiny area of the house not modernized and renovated. The walls to either side are still the original, exposed brick from the home's construction in the 1920's. The brick of the far wall is light red and uniform; but the wall behind me, above my bedroom, is tarnished black with ash and soot, as if scorched.

"Hello?" I whisper in the void of silence. My breath forms ghosts of mist in the bitter air. "Hello? Walter?" I rise to my feet and step into the attic. The cold makes me shiver and clutch myself. I start to cross on tiptoe toward the small window on the far side, the floorboards frigid on my bare feet.

"Are you here?" I whisper again.

Something creeks behind me and I spin around. The rocking chair at the back of the room has begun to rock by itself. Simultaneously, the old yellow newspapers stacked against the wall begin to fly, circling through the air like birds. I try to contain my fear. Walter has not attempted to physically harm us—not yet.

"*Bitch!*" a voice booms in my ear. "*I warned you!*"

My heart lurches and I turn around again—but there's nothing there. The air is so cold it stings my throat as I gasp for breath. "Please," I whisper. "I just want to talk."

"*I told you people,*" rasps the voice on the air, "*to get out.*"

The newspapers flap and swirl like they're caught in a cyclone, beating against me.

"*Do you know WHAT I AM?*"

"Stop!" I fall to my knees, shielding my face from the onslaught of flying objects. "Please, Walter! *Stop!*"

The papers flutter to the floor like dead leaves. The rocking chair slowly comes to a stop. I look up, sniffing and blinking like an owl in the dark. The room seems still and empty again.

Then a soft voice speaks behind me, more corporeal than before: "There's nothing left to be said."

I turn, and in the far corner, shaded from the thin light of the window, a dark shape crouches, its back bent to me. It hugs itself with long, slender limbs, its shoulders hitching as if weeping—or laughing.

"I warned you it would get worse," it whispers in a thin, reedy voice. "I told you..." Its back starts to hitch. It's rising to its feet.

I take a step back, starting to breathe again in little soft gasps, skin prickling under my pajamas.

It turns, grinning, the lips and gums burnt back to expose huge white teeth, filling its black and ruined face. Thin tufts of hair poke up from its great round skull. It starts to utter a hoarse panting grunt like an animal's warning, its bony hackles rising, and I back away, too late.

The burned thing lunges, its great teeth gnashing for my throat.

I scream and hunch aside, and something *pushes* me from behind and I lose my balance, sprawling to the floor at the edge of the stairs. I hunch up, shielding my head with my hands—but only a very cold wind passes overhead, cold enough to sting my skin. The apparition is gone.

"You should go," says the voice, now soft and child-like. "Before I hurt you."

When I look up the rocking chair in the back is moving again—but this time it's occupied by someone, rocking slowly in the shadows. Darkness surrounds the figure like fog, writhing and tendrilous.

As if from far away, I hear Mom shouting faintly downstairs, still fighting. "You *let* them do it! You always *let* them push you around and then take it out on *us!*"

"Like I had a choice!" Dad's voice sounds broken. "It was move or severance. I thought I'd be buying at the *bottom*... I thought, how could prices get any lower?"

Shaking my head, I push myself up onto hands and knees. "No, Walter," I whisper, utterly without force. "I can't let this go on."

The figure in the chair stops rocking, and stands.

"Listen," I say pleadingly. "I know you want us to go—"

"I want my *old* family back," the figure interrupts, his voice petulant, thin as a blade. "I *hate* you people! So loud, so… obnoxious. You need to go. Before I *kill* you!"

I remain on my knees, looking up at the figure. The moonlight cannot reach the back of the room where he stands. "Believe me, we *want* to go," I try again. "But, all this trouble… it's actually keeping us here *longer*."

"I know you're just trying to *sell* it," Walter responds, "and I don't want that either! I want my old family—them, or no one!"

"You mean… the people the bank kicked out?" I ask.

"*Shut up!*" the figure shrieks, and the walls of the attic creak and groan. "Don't you talk about them!"

"Please!" I clasp my hands. "Please, Walter!"

"Why do you keep *calling* me that?"

I pause, taken aback. Earnestly, I answer, "When I looked up our house, I found your name. From 1998. Boy, eleven, killed in residential fire. That was you, wasn't it?"

The figure takes one step closer, and the moonlight suddenly reaches one side of its face—and that side is a young boy's face, fresh and bright-eyed, empty of expression. The other side, where the moonlight does not land, looks black and burnt beyond recognition.

"If I can get my dad to sell the house back to the old people, will you leave us alone?" I ask. "Will you stop wrecking the house and causing us grief, if I promise to get them back here?"

Slowly, the visible portion of Walter's face begins to smile.

Later, when I tell my parents, they don't like the idea. Mom can't stop crying over the thought that I actually talked to the demon. Dad says if the previous owners couldn't afford the house before, they won't be able to now—and since they've got a foreclosure on their records, the bank would never approve the sale. I press him to at least try, and finally he relents.

Walter keeps his end of the deal. For the next week, the house lies dormant. The tranquility seems almost unusual now, and Mom and Dad can't believe it. By the end of the week, the mood of the house has turned around completely. I can't relax, however. Though there are no more overt disturbances, I can still hear Walter stirring at night in the attic, tapping the floorboards above my bed with a clawed finger, reminding me he's waiting. And I can't shake the last thing he said to me, after agreeing to my peace offering that night.

"Girl—nothing's holding me here, except my own will. If you betray me, or fail me in any way, I will hunt you down. I can follow you to the ends of the Earth."

Each morning I remind my parents about the urgency of finding the previous owners. Having seen the peace taking hold as I promised, Dad is taking the task seriously. By the weekend, the private investigator he's hired forwards us contact information for one Ms. Brenda Lee Tanner.

Mom and Dad never mention how they pay the private eye, but I notice the same day that Mom's diamond-encrusted engagement ring has vanished from her hand, and her eyes seem especially bleary and far away.

To Dad's surprise, Ms. Tanner is enthusiastic to receive his call, and she flies in to see the house almost before Dad can ask. She arrives Tuesday evening with a skinny bald man in a three-piece suit and an elderly woman with thinning hair—her lawyer and her realtor, respectively. Brenda Tanner is old as well, with greying hair tugged back in a bun and thick glasses. She is short and heavyset, with a distinct forward bend to her back that, combined with her serene smile, lends her a certain endearing subservience.

She smooths her skirts as she sits on the couch, gazing around at her former home with misty eyes. I watch from the foot of the stairs, on the far side of the living room.

"I can't thank you folks enough," Ms. Tanner whispers, her voice thin and rough as powdered glass. "Goin' to the trouble of finding me, setting right the bank's wrong…"

Ms. Tanner, flanked by the bald lawyer and the elderly realtor on the couch, dabs her wrinkled eyes with an embroidered handkerchief. "Actually," she sighs, "this place has a lot of history for me. We meant to pay off the mortgage, grow old and retire here, but one thing led to another and… after the fire, things were never quite the same."

"So there *was* a fire," Dad says.

Tanner blinks back at him. "The banks didn't tell you?"

The bald lawyer clears his throat and intones, "Unless it relates to the current condition, they are not required to disclose past damage." The elderly realtor smiles and nods.

"Well, there was a fire all right," Ms. Tanner continues, a rueful smile creasing her face. It takes her a moment to continue. "Ted—my ex-husband—he blamed himself for what happened. Started drinking heavy again. Eventually he lost his job, and... well..."

Dad nods gravely, holding Mom close to him on the loveseat. In a gentle voice he says, "Well, if you want the house back..."

"I saw the list price," Tanner says. "Even less than they wanted from us back then." She smiles thinly. "The bank won't approve me for a loan, but hell—I can pay cash. My husband's life insurance saw to that."

I breathe a huge sigh of relief. Everything's going as planned. Walter's old family will return to the house, where they belong, and my family will be left in peace. Mom and Dad exchange glances on the loveseat, smiling, holding hands.

Then Ms. Tanner leans back, her smile now shrewd. "Except, I can only afford about forty thousand less than you're asking."

When Tanner leaves, Dad is furious, pacing through the living room, pulling on his already thin hair. He spends the next two days on the phone with the bank, trying to make them accept Tanner's low-ball offer. When he's not on the phone, he's back to shouting at Mom or glaring at the TV with a glass of scotch in hand. It's the greedy banks, Mom explains. They refuse to take less than their asking price.

Things start happening in the house again—just minor things, like the paint in the basement resuming its peeling, and electronics inexplicably shorting out—and I warn them Walter is growing impatient.

Finally one day I come home from school to find Dad at the kitchen table with his head in his hands, weeping. Mom smiles tentatively and offers me a Coke. "The banks accepted," she says. "Dad's going to cover the difference, just so we can get out."

In order to do this, Dad has to deplete his 401k, some account he's been saving up since he first started working. I don't know why he's so upset. At least Walter is satisfied, I tell him. This does little to cheer him.

And in another three weeks I'm looking on the living room for

the final time, saying goodbye (and good riddance). All our things—
what we didn't pawn for cash—are packed and waiting in the truck, and
the little cape cod seems cold and empty.

Ms. Tanner arrives, all smiles, to take the house keys.

"Well," says Mom, barely hiding her gloating, "enjoy your new
home."

And Ms. Tanner laughs.

"No, honey, I *got* a home." She points back to her Mercedes,
idling on the curb behind Dad's truck. "I live with my new hubby back
in New York. Isn't he handsome?" An old man with thick white hair
waves from the driver's seat.

"You mean you're not moving in?" I say with dismay. "But
the… the house *wants* you back!"

Tanner looks back at me, expressionless. "We lost a child in the
fire," she murmurs. "I could *never* live here again." She sniffs, gazes at
the aluminum siding almost contemptuously. "I only bought this for
rental income."

"Rental income?" I exclaim.

"There's the college right down the road," Ms. Tanner says,
addressing my parents now. "And it's a great spot for commuters. I
might even convert the upstairs to a separate apartment… finish out the
attic…"

"No!" I cry, grabbing the old woman's dress. "That's not what
we agreed to!"

Both Mom and Dad move to pull me back, apologizing
profusely.

"You're supposed to live here again!" I go on shouting. "You
can't just… rent it to some college kids!"

"Come on, dear." Mom leads me toward Dad's old Ford.

If you betray me, or fail me in any way—

"That's not what Walter wants!" I shout at Tanner.

Tanner looks back with bewilderment—no doubt trying to recall
when she'd mentioned her son's name to us—but by then Mom is
shoving me into the back seat of the car. She quiets me with a warning
look. "Don't say anything that might screw this up!" she hisses. "Not

when we might finally get out of this!"

I stare up at the windows of the house. In my former bedroom window, for a moment, I believe I see a face, glaring down at the yard.

Then it's gone.

I watch the house fade in the distance as we drive toward the local motel where we stayed before. "This isn't what Walter wanted," I tell them anxiously.

"Don't worry, honey," says Dad, adjusting the rear-view mirror. "We've got plenty else to worry about now, but not that. Say goodbye, babe. That nightmare's over."

But my foreboding does not diminish. As we drive, I notice all the exterior house-lights and street lamps seem to flicker or wink out as our car passes by. And I can sense the presence of something, sitting next to me in the backseat, an invisible fourth passenger, sullen and cold as ice. Turning his burnt face toward me.

And grinning.

About the Author

A.E. Hodge is an up-and-coming fiction writer. His first collection of short fiction is entitled *Spoiled Lunch and Other Creepy Tales (2013)*. His next work, a novella entitled *So Damn Beautiful*, is expected in late 2013.

Hodge has a personal website at **www.aehodge.com**. He maintains a blog entitled "Fiction Fugitive", where he offers advice on building wealth and escaping the rat race by making income as a writer, living frugally, and generating passive income streams. You can also follow him on Facebook (A.E. Hodge) and Twitter (@FictionFugitive).

Hodge is a graduate of the University of Maryland, Baltimore County. He lives outside Baltimore, Maryland.

Also By A.E. Hodge:

So Damn Beautiful: A Novella (forthcoming, 2013)

Spoiled Dinner: More Creepy Tales (forthcoming, TBD)

SO YOU WANT TO BE A WRITER...?

Let's face it: it's not easy to make a living as a writer. Living expenses are high, pay is low, publishers are picky, and the daily grind of the rat race consumes most of your time and energy. If only you could *retire extremely early* from your day job and *make a living* as a *full-time writer*!

Sound too good to be true?

FICTION FUGITIVE
www.fictionfugitive.com
The Official Blog of A.E. Hodge
Fiction. Finance. Freedom.

- **Learn how to escape the rat race through a combination of fiction writing, frugal living, and income investing**
- **Peek inside the life of a self-published writer and get insider tips on writing, publishing, and marketing fiction**
- **Connect with other writers, practice the craft, and get feedback on your work**
- **Find your own path to financial security as a full-time writer**

Interested? Check out **Fiction Fugitive** today!

www.fictionfugitive.com

www.ingramcontent.com/pod-product-compliance
Lightning Source LLC
Chambersburg PA
CBHW070459130626
46555CB00003B/1069